COMING HOME

COMING
HOME

Stories from the Northwest Territories

foreword
BY RICHARD VAN CAMP

ENFIELD
&WIZENTY

Enfield & Wizenty
(An imprint of Great Plains Publications)
345-955 Portage Avenue
Winnipeg, MB R3G OP9
www.greatplains.mb.ca

Great Plains Publications gratefully acknowledges the financial support provided for its publishing program by the Government of Canada through the Canada Book Fund; the Canada Council for the Arts; the Province of Manitoba through the Book Publishing Tax Credit and the Book Publisher Marketing Assistance Program; and the Manitoba Arts Council.

Design & Typography by Relish New Brand Experience Inc.
Printed in Canada by Friesens
Cover photograph by Dave Brosha

Publication of this Anthology made possible with funding from De Beers Canada Inc.

LIBRARY AND ARCHIVES CANADA CATALOGUING IN PUBLICATION

Coming home : stories from the Northwest Territories /
foreword by Richard Van Camp.

ISBN 978-1-926531-27-4

1. Canadian literature (English)--Northwest Territories. 2. Canadian literature (English)--21st century.

PS8255.N57C66 2012   C810'.8097193   C2012-903585-8

FSC
www.fsc.org

MIX
Paper from
responsible sources
FSC® C016245

ENVIRONMENTAL BENEFITS STATEMENT

Great Plains Publications saved the following resources by printing the pages of this book on chlorine free paper made with 100% post-consumer waste.

TREES	WATER	ENERGY	SOLID WASTE	GREENHOUSE GASES
7	3,305	3	209	733
FULLY GROWN	GALLONS	MILLION BTUs	POUNDS	POUNDS

Environmental impact estimates were made using the Environmental Paper Network Paper Calculator. For more information visit www.papercalculator.org.

Table of Contents

Introduction

De Beers Canada

The stories we tell reveal much about who we are. Through words we express our hopes and dreams, explore our emotions and capture a snapshot of a time and a place. For readers, stories fuel our imaginations, taking us on a journey of understanding and exploration, helping us experience the world through someone else's eyes.

At De Beers Canada, we know the Northwest Territories and the people who live here have many stories to share with the world. We're honoured to be able to help northerners share their stories through this anthology, a partnership with NorthWords NWT.

How this collection came to happen is a story in itself. De Beers believes literacy is the first step in empowering people to shape their own future and that it is a key to ensuring individual opportunities, community development, and economic success.

From this passion for education grew our Books in Homes program. Each year since 2003 we have encouraged students in Aboriginal communities close to our projects to read, with a gift of three books. In 2012, the program marks ten years and will reach a significant milestone—distribution of over 30,000 books in the NWT alone. Since then, this program has expanded to include students living near the Victor Mine in Northern Ontario.

Our support for literacy has also included support for projects in the Northwest Territories and Ontario.

As Premier Sponsor of NorthWords, we helped nurture the dream of an annual festival to become a thriving, year-round celebration of writing and writers.

Through this anthology, our partnership with NorthWords takes a new, exciting step forward. Congratulations to everyone who submitted works for consideration.

We hope that the stories you find on these pages take you on an unforgettable journey, where you discover something about the Northwest Territories and, perhaps, learn something about yourself as well.

About De Beers Canada:
De Beers Canada is Canada's leading diamond company, operating the Snap Lake Mine, the Victor Mine, the Gahcho Kué Project and De Beers Canada Exploration, with offices in Toronto, Timmins and Yellowknife. De Beers Canada is also part of the De Beers Family of Companies, which has been exploring for diamonds in Canada for more than 50 years and opened its first mines in Canada in 2008. De Beers Canada employs approximately 1,000 people across the country and, through the Snap Lake and Victor Mines, provides ten percent, by value, of diamonds to the secondary industry in the Northwest Territories and Ontario respectively. All De Beers' Canadian production is sold under contract to the Diamond Trading Company (DTC) in the United Kingdom. For more information, please visit www.debeerscanada.com.

Foreword

by Richard Van Camp

Welcome!

I was told once that in the eleven official languages of the Northwest Territories, "fire" is often the same word for "home." I can believe it. In these stories, there's a lot of fire and a whole lotta home. I'm proud to say I know most of these authors you're about to read and—*hoo!*—do they bring the heat in what they've gathered for you and for all of us who discover this treasure, this first of firsts for the north. There has never been an anthology like this before, and we are all so proud and grateful to be a part of it.

Like all great literature, it's a bit of a hike, hey? We're gonna lead you to the top of the Butte in the Deh Cho Region and we're going to welcome you through five worlds (the traditional, the dream, the spirit, the historical and the now). We've got some sexy for you as in Annelies Pool's *Celia's Inner Anorexic*. There are a few ghost stories in here, as in Cathy Jewison's *Haunted Hill Mine,* and we'll lead you in and around the city of Yellowknife. You're going to get cagey with cabin fever in January Go's *For Us* and you'll be attending a rowdy house party with Shawn McCann in *The Long Gun*. Unfortunately, you're going to do a little time in the pokey with Patti-Kay Hamilton's *Jailbird* and possibly with the characters from Christine Raves's *Dirty Rascal.*

Heartbreak walks through my hometown of Fort Smith in *Born a Girl*, through the fictional town of the Stew in *The Points* by Colin Henderson and rests with a family near Sachs Harbour in Cara Loverock's *Homecoming.*

You'll be on the land, the water, in dreams. We have fish, fish and more fish in Brian Penney's soul-dizzying *Ts'ankui Theda, The*

Kindness of the Lake, and you'll share an epiphany with Rebecca Aylward out on the land of her ancestors.

There is the terror of first contact from both sides in Jordan Carpenter's story *Finding Home* and *Angatkuq* by Marcus Jackson, and you'll revisit, through the eyes of a child and narrated by Jamesie Fournier, the violent labour dispute of the '90s that stuck the north's capital city. You are holding so much northern spirit in your hands, right here, right now. The Land of the Midnight Sun is shining in all of these stories and we hope you love it.

The best part of reading this anthology for me? Being blown away by people I thought I knew and seeing them shine in a new way. Jessie C. MacKenzie's *Where They Belong* made my soul dance. I'll never forget Colin Henderson's last line. I thought I knew Patti-Kay Hamilton but her story was such a surprise and Dave Brosha's cover? Brilliant!

Coming Home is a testament to the beauty of the land, the communities and the people who choose to live here. Welcome and *mahsi cho.* Thank you so very much for joining us.

Richard Van Camp
Tlicho Dene from Fort Smith, NWT

Fiction

The Points

by Colin Henderson

started working at the General at the beginning of grade ten. My parents were talking about sending me to college in southern Canada, and about how expensive that would be. I couldn't see that far ahead but I knew I needed the money and a way to pass the time. The most abundant resource in Fort Steward is time. Here in the Stew, population south of 1,000 and dropping, it's all just a matter of time.

On the Thursday after last class, at the start of summer holidays, Sean and Anthony walk into the General.

Since starting at the store, I haven't been around much for Sean. He's my bro in every way that matters. We met in grade three, when my family first moved to the Stew. Our teacher had assigned us to work together on a report about muskoxen. Back then Sean was playing the part of little shit in class and always getting beaten up at recess. While presenting our report, he said the teacher smelled like a muskox. I never laughed so hard in my life. We've been close ever since. Sean usually tries but he's not very good at anything. He's almost useless in the bush, which is why his parents left him behind this summer when they went out on the land. He pretends it's awesome because they left him their truck and gave him $500. But he knows they've given up on him and that really hurts.

I walk around the till and meet Sean in the aisle. When I raise my hand, he slaps it. We both swing our heads back and snap our fingers, our imitation of Will and Jazz from the reruns of Fresh Prince we used to watch as kids. It's been years and we still shake hands the same way.

"Partying tonight?" Sean says.

I nod. I know he's buying because of the money.

Anthony and Sean have been hanging out lately. Sean's friend has just witnessed our ceremony with a puzzled look. I don't know if he's ever watched TV. Anthony lives at the Points, a dozen miles east of town, on a ranch without livestock. Life at the Points is one of the Stew's great mysteries.

Everyone knows parts of the story. Anthony's grandfather, arriving in the north seventy years ago, a decade too late for Yellowknife's gold rush, had no luck panning gold where the Points Rapids choke the Steward River. So he set to raising cattle. In the floodplains. The old man and his cockeyed schemes have long since passed, replaced by Anthony's father, a man who recognized the Points as an ideal fishing spot. (The Dene had known this for years). And somehow, despite the abundant whitefish and pickerel, Anthony's family is still one of the poorest in the Stew.

"Hook me up with some smokes?" he says.

"I can't." My boss keeps tight inventory and has his camera pointed at the till. Handing Anthony a pack would cost my job.

"Brendan is booting tonight. He just wants something for his troubles."

Outside, waiting for them, is the meanest drunk in the Stew. Brendan is twenty-one and still hangs around the high school sometimes, showing off his truck and beating up kids.

I don't know if Anthony knows how much money Sean actually has, because if I were Sean I wouldn't tell him, and because Sean needs the rest of the money for groceries. All Anthony owns is a shitty tenspeed. So I offer some money to cover Brendan's fee.

Anthony follows me to the back of the store, to the ATM. I take out $20. But Brendan will have to come in and buy the pack since the rest of us are just sixteen and the cameras are still rolling.

The guys walk outside to Brendan's truck and hand him the money.

He comes in and offers my bill for a pack of smokes. He's got this scar under his right eye from a fight that happened longer back than I can remember. I know not to stare at it. Instead I look past him, past the DVDs, where we have a movie poster for *No Country for Old Men*.

I feel like the gas station attendant dealing with Anton Chigurh. Brendan knows I'm afraid to look him in the eye.

"Can I help you?" he says, like he's the one serving me.

I force myself to look at him and say, "The regular kind?"

Brendan breathes deeply. I can hear his breath reach the back of his throat. He is staring at me.

He comes into the General every day and follows a similar routine. I know he'll scowl if I give him the pack with the inflamed lung or the limp-dick cigarette. He scowls less when I hand him the pack with children complaining about second-hand smoke.

"You've been friendly with Nat?" he says. "Hopefully not too friendly."

He is talking about his sister, this girl I've been in love with since like forever. I watch Nat in class and guess whether she's going to raise her hand that day, or how many times she'll tuck her hair behind her ears. She's always biting her pens. And she smiles less on Mondays and Fridays, on the days that bookend the weekends. We sometimes talk in the hallway. But there's no way he can know how much I like her.

I nod and lock the twenty in the cash register. We now have the pack and the change on the counter between us.

My boss keeps a baseball bat behind the till. I glance at the movie poster again. If Brendan starts talking about "standing to win everything" on a coin flip, I will reach for the bat and keep swinging until I can't swing anymore.

A few moments later, when Brendan leaves the store, he takes my change with him. I feel sorry for Nat, but I also have to think about myself now and again.

That night there is a party behind the pump house. We are sitting to the side on some concrete blocks away from the crowd. Anthony is telling Sean and me about stealing $300 from a house on Olsen Crescent.

"These people know I did it," he says. "They're threatening to press charges, to send me to jail."

Sean says, "That sucks."

I'm buzzing from the gin and thinking about when Anthony was younger. He used to show up to elementary school every day smelling like fish and sweat, with the same lunch—bread, butter, fried whitefish—and alternating black eyes. He stopped coming after we started high school. And yet he still bikes to town every morning, down the same unpaved highway on the same shitty ten-speed without a seat. Something is drawing him to the Stew. Or something is driving him from the Points.

"What are you going to do?" I say.

"They say I can pay them back and they won't press charges. But their money is gone. And if dad finds out, he'll kill me."

I don't ask why he broke into the house, because I think I understand. Nor do I ask where the money went because all that matters is that it's gone.

"That sucks," Sean says again, and I realize he's thinking about giving Anthony his grocery money. Instead, Anthony asks me for it.

When I was grabbing the money for Brendan, Anthony saw my bank balance. He knows I have $1,000. But I worked hard, taking shit from customers like Brendan. And I need that money as much as Anthony does. We both want to buy our way out of prisons.

Sean is ready to starve for Anthony's safety. I'm still thinking back to elementary school, remembering what Sean was like, getting chased around the schoolyard at recess. And now I remember, too, that Anthony has stuck up for Sean more than once.

"Okay," I say, finally.

Anthony's face lights up. He offers me a shot of the gin Sean paid for.

I excuse myself and trudge off into the bush, looking for a place to piss. Nat is away from the party too, sitting alone against a stump of spruce.

"Are you okay?" I say.

"Yeah, Chris," she says, and she stands up. "I'm just going home."

I can see that she's buzzing and readying herself to walk home through a bush path that comes out on the other side of town, one block from her house.

"You shouldn't go it alone," I say.

I step away to relieve myself. A few moments later, when I return, I find Nat still there. She asks if she can tell me something.

As I walk her home, Nat repeatedly swears me to secrecy. She tells me that last Thursday Brendan had passed out on the couch, covered in blood. She says she held a mirror to his face to see if he was breathing. She wetted a facecloth and wiped him clean, searching his body for puncture wounds.

"Thank God he wasn't hurt. I wonder about the other guy."

Nat is worried that Brendan won't make it back home from one of his fights. Their parents are in this crazy dysfunctional marriage. She needs Brendan, she says, because he's the only one who understands her.

Without thinking, I say, "I want to understand you, too."

She pauses and sweeps her hair behind her ear.

She tucks her head into my shoulder, and stays like that for a long time.

I'm back at the General in the morning. Nat stops in to thank me for walking her home and listening to her.

"You owe me one of your secrets," she says.

I don't know why but I tell her about Anthony wanting to borrow money.

"Have you given it to him?" she says.

I pat my chest pocket, which is usually empty. I say, "I had to wait for the bank to open. Anthony should be stopping by soon enough."

She asks if I knew her dad was a friend of Anthony's father. And that Brendan used to work at the Points in the summers, catching fish.

She says, "Brendan thinks Anthony reminds him of himself. Sometimes we let Anthony stay on our couch, when shit is too rough at his house."

Nat tells me this story about how Anthony used to steal her notebooks in kindergarten and doodle all over them. He would draw princesses in castles and tell her that was her life. She says, "You know he still likes me, right?"

Five minutes later, Nat is still around. Anthony shows up at the General with Sean. He asks again for the money.

I wonder if jealousy is impacting my decision when I tell him, "I can't."

"You can't or you won't?" he says.

"Both."

Anthony shakes his head and storms out, knocking over a display of DVDs on the way. Sean follows him and they head toward Sean's house. Before they leave the property, I can see Anthony kicking over a garbage can that I'm going to have to clean up.

It's obvious that I've made a lifelong enemy.

Sean calls me that night. He's frantic. The money his parents left him, the $500 that was supposed to cover a whole summer's worth of groceries, is missing.

Days pass.

Sean and I are walking to a party at Phil's, this guy who lives on Ruben Street. Playing catch up, we take shots from a mickey and stop behind the high school to smoke a joint. When we arrive at the party, Nat is waiting in the kitchen to argue Anthony's case.

"Not a chance he stole it," she says.

"Nothing has ever gone missing before," I say. "Would Sean rob himself?"

She looks at him. "Maybe you misplaced it."

Sean says, "Yeah, right. Maybe it grew legs."

I leave them in the kitchen and head into the living room. I find Anthony sitting in a crowd, talking about Sean. He spots me and raises his voice.

"Telling people I stole his stupid money? Next time I see him, he's dead."

Anthony is baiting me but I don't know if I can take him. And I know that being high isn't helping my side.

The host, Phil, asks if I want a beer. I follow him into the kitchen. He urges me to leave with Sean, who is still arguing with Nat.

I part them and say to Sean, "We need to jet."

Out on Ruben Street a few minutes later, we are walking to his house.

"Anthony is such a fucker," Sean says. "Stealing my money and wanting to kick my ass too. What kind of person does that?"

I shake my head. I don't know. Nor do I know what to do about him.

It's Saturday. I'm working at the General again.

Nat calls to tell me something. "After you left, I went outside for a cigarette and to clear my head. Anthony followed me out and put his arm around me, trying to comfort me."

She pauses for a breath. "You won't say anything to my brother?"

"Yeah." I can't imagine any scenario where I willingly approach Brendan.

"Anthony kissed me. I tried to stop him, but I couldn't." Now I need a breath.

"I wasn't kissing back. And so finally he stopped. And he had this look I had never seen before. He was holding my hands and not let-ting go. I yelled at him, which must have snapped him back. He looked really scared and he let me go and he said he was just playing."

"He attacked you?" I say.

"He was drunk. He got carried away. I don't know why I told you." I hang up on her. I'm not mad at her for what's happened, but I'm mad that she put herself in that position.

I grab the baseball bat from behind the till and shut down the General early. I walk toward Sean's house. When I get there, I rally him. We have a couple shots, grab the keys to his parents' truck and ride out, like two gunslingers.

We need to find Anthony. Better us than Brendan.

I'm driving Sean's truck. Sean says Anthony won't be at the Points. It's the last place he'll go.

There are only so many places to hide in the Stew. There's a cabin out at Green Lake. Anthony isn't there. Nor is he at the wildfire-spotting tower. Back in town, we check the arcade. We can only think of one more place to look.

The Stew is barely north of sixty. It's ten and starting to darken. I park the truck a block from the water pumping station and get out, quietly closing the doors so as not to startle Anthony. We are guided by light from the aurora and a near-vacant moon.

Anthony's shitty ten-speed is parked at the side of the building. With the money he has stolen, I would expect him to replace the missing seat.

He's sitting on the concrete blocks, waiting out back for Sean and me.

"I'm sorry," he says.

"I would have given you that money," Sean says. "You just had to ask."

"I'm sick of asking for everything," Anthony says.

I might feel sympathetic, if not for what he did to Nat.

I take a big swing at Anthony's face but he moves and so I catch him instead below his right eye. He bolts past my second swing and bowls over Sean. I chase him but trip.

Anthony reaches his bike and rides away on the nearest bush trail. This time we know where he's going. Anthony is a heat-seeking missile aimed at the corner of Ruben and Olsen, a block from Nat's house. Sean and I want to intercept him before he delivers himself to Brendan.

We arrive before Anthony and park the truck.

Sean says, "He didn't need all of my money." The situation with Nat is similar. He already had her friendship.

Anthony emerges, not from the trail's end but instead from the brush nearer Nat's. He scrambles to the house and drops his bike in the driveway, beside Brendan's truck.

Sean and I get out of our truck. But we stop moving when Brendan walks out his front door. His eyes are bloodshot and watery. Again he reminds me of Anton Chigurh. He's ready to kill someone.

He says, "Tonight the action is coming to me?" Nat appears behind Brendan.

"They think Anthony stole some money," she says.

"He ripped me off," Sean says.

"It wasn't him," Nat says. She has an undying faith that I will never understand.

Everyone else is watching Brendan, like a judge ready to render a verdict. But Nat is watching me. She shakes her head almost imperceptibly, trying not to catch anyone's attention other than mine. She is not going to tell Brendan what happened with Anthony. And she needs me to keep my mouth shut too.

"One warning," Brendan says. "Leave now." Something in Brendan's voice suggests if I rat he will kill Anthony, but also that he'll kick the shit out of us too, and maybe Nat.

"This is between us and Anthony," I say. I'm still next to Sean's truck. I reach into the box and feel the handle of the baseball bat. I lift it up so Brendan can understand that I'm serious about taking Anthony.

Brendan almost smiles. "Pull it out and I'll shove it up your ass," he says. He's serious too. And so I drop the bat. It hits hard and rattles around the box for a few seconds.

Sean and I stay back, but we aren't leaving. Anthony has this beating coming to him. There is only so far you can push things.

"Leave. Please." Nat mouths these words to me. I look at her blankly.

So she begs Brendan to drive Anthony home. Brendan tells us not to move.

"When I come back you better be here waiting." Brendan lifts Anthony's shitty ten-speed and throws it in the box of his truck. He chuckles, now noticing that Anthony doesn't have a seat on his bike.

Anthony is jumping into the passenger seat, looking relieved and scared. If I didn't know better, I would think he was readying himself to confess everything.

Brendan backs out and nearly runs over Sean's toe. Yet neither of us moves. Brendan says to Sean, "Good for you, little shit."

He points at me and says, "I shall return." Our last sight of them is driving up Ruben and turning left.

I wish I could say what happened when Brendan returned. I wish I could say how Sean and I got beat down. Trust me, I do.

The dirt highway heading to the Points is twisty. Brendan was barrelling along at whatever fucking speed and overshot the last turn. They skidded off the road, flipped once, and collided with a granite mound that existed thousands of years before Anthony's grandfather came up the Steward River, a decade too late for Yellowknife's gold rush.

Anthony's shitty ten-speed was flung into a stand of birch trees.

The truck leaked gas and exploded.

Nat is haunted. That's what her friends have told me, since she never talks to me anymore. She has nightmares about Anthony crawling out of the truck, seeing Brendan disabled and the vehicle overturned, leaning against the wreckage, not smelling the leaking gas, lighting a cigarette, killing them both. She wakes up every morning to a cold sweat.

But we are all haunted. Sean beats himself up about being too scared to move when Brendan nearly ran him over. He would give anything to have that moment back.

There were so many decision points. Who knows what would have happened if I had leant Anthony that money. Or if Sean had. Or if Nat hadn't told me about Anthony.

The moment I'm haunted by, the one that plays over in my head, is reaching for the baseball bat. I could have pulled it out of the box. Then only Sean and I would have been beaten. Or maybe Nat would have come to her senses and told Brendan the whole story.

Then maybe Anthony would be the only one dead.

I think about my choice unceasingly. I can feel the bat, the weight of it. I grip the handle. No matter how hard I try, I still feel the bat slipping out of my hand, still see it falling back into place, still hear it rattling around in the box of Sean's truck.

And I still let it go. Every time.

COLIN HENDERSON, author of *The Points*, spent his child-hood in Fort Smith and his teen years in Yellowknife. Throughout university, while working towards a busi-ness degree, he spent much of his free time creative writing. Then in 2008, after five years spent working in Whitehorse, Colin took a break from his marketing career. His experiences in the north had provided an undeni-able creative inspiration. He has since written two novels—*Reason and Doubt* and *Yukonian Knights*—that he hopes to publish in the coming years. *The Points* is his first published work.

Finding Home

by Jordan Carpenter

I can't remember the face of Uumma. I try to think of what her hands felt like to hold them, how her skin felt on my lips, the scent she had on her breath, the words she spoke to me before I left on their *qayavialuk*. Nothing. I can remember nothing. I am staring at the floor, with all its cracks and rot and dirt and blood and it reminds me that I am in their world now. There is a stench coming from the other side of this room—this hole—like a rotting seal corpse. Flies are buzzing constantly, nearly drowning out the noise of the water slamming itself against one of the walls, like hundreds of muted drums, beating randomly. For every great thump from the waves, water oozes in through the massive logs like blood, quietly and slowly onto the damp floor. The water flows to the corner of the stench, collecting under the body of Mirayualuk, allowing the things which feast on his body to grow larger and eat faster, and I am thankful for it.

Mirayualuk. He is the reason I am in this hole. The reason why I wait for a *tunik* to feed me. The reason why I cannot remember her. I want him to be gone from this world as quickly as the animals will allow. I wish I could see the maggots crawl in and out of his eyes, to watch as spiders and flies fight for a place to nest in his mouth, to see him suffer, writhe, scream, die. He was being eaten by the bugs before they took me onto their *qayavialuk*, but even if he was still alive, it is too dark to see anything beyond the reflection of the water and gleam of the metal from the barrels and plates at my feet.

I cannot remember the last time I ate, and the thought makes me realize how hungry I am. They have been feeding me a tough, dark meat and strange chewy, white balls; they call it "bread." They have an odd language; it is not from deep within themselves that they call their words, but from somewhere on the surface of their tongue. These balls are filling, but I want *natchiq* and *pipsi*, the meats I had at home. I want to be the one to feed Uumma, to not depend on our relations for hunting, to show her I have lived up to my name.

A noise comes from beyond the hole's walls. Muffled whispering. "The man … get … the room." Drowsy footsteps wander towards the door. Strange noises come from the door suddenly, like two rocks clashing together which stop as abruptly as they started. A *tunik* appears. His mere existence in this hole makes me want to kill, but I know he is my source of food and only way to find Uumma. The light from the midnight sky makes everything glow, and seems to animate the corpse, the hole and myself; all decrepit, all dying, all dead. I bathe in the fresh air.

"Oh … God." He chokes on the odour, spits. "Come, with haste. Food." He makes a gesture with his hand. Using the rough, jagged sacks around me as grips, I attempt to hoist myself and fail. Crumpling to the ground, I realize my muscles are like the *nuvatqiq* that wash on the shore—the ones without bones. I look to the door for help, but the man has already left. My want to hurt him gives me the energy to leave this hole.

Outside my hole, there are other holes, but they are empty and smell worse than even mine. Knowing this makes me feel a small glow in my chest I have not felt in many days.

"You! Come!" My head jerks right and I am overwhelmed by the moon's sharp glow shooting in from behind the man. I cower, covering my eyes. A fear strikes me, forcing me to remember the last days.

"Angunayuak!" Mirayualuk's voice cuts through the village's noise, straight into my ears and jerks me out of my hunting practice. It is shrill like a gull, piercing. He knows better, yet I endure his presence; he seems to always say something that might matter. I set down the bow, turning to him as he sprints towards me. His pitiful legs are almost too fast for his small body to keep up.

"*Angiyuq! Angiyuq qayavialuk!*" he screams, pointing towards the great water. I notice the village turning. A hush moves its way through the people as they gaze at this massive brown ship passing by. The children throw their legs in front of them as fast as they can, rushing to the shore to call at the ship, with the mothers swiftly behind, snatching them up and carrying them back to the animal-skin tents.

The ship is larger than anything I have ever seen, made of entire trees. I cannot imagine anywhere with so many trees. Those that have lived through the most winters have a slight look of concern strike their face, yet quickly revert to their expressionless masks when our eyes meet. For them to worry would cause the entire village to worry.

The commotion must have woken Uumma, as she stands next to her mother with her hair frizzled and random, with that forever puzzled face. I know that she finds the commotion disturbing to her sleep; nothing could be so important as to wake her. Along with her confused face, a very delicate touch of both annoyance and worry rest on her face, and these restrained fears worry me as well. Thankfully, she notices me and her entire face eases into pure joy, as does mine. We lock eyes: they are as thin as the rocks that skip on the water the best, always thankful and happy. I catch myself mesmerized, become aware again and she laughs. I laugh too, and know I am in love.

Some of the villagers laugh, pointing to the ocean. I turn to see that, like the children, Mirayualuk is rushing to shore to see the ship in its entirety. As they run, the ship—somehow—turns its huge body towards us, as if it is a great beast looking for a hunt. The looming creature frightens both the children and Mirayualuk, who all scamper quickly towards the village. To see the enormous girth of this ship surveying us— seemingly judging the weakest of us to pursue, like the wolf does with the caribou—startles me and the villagers as well. Something so large yet able to glide across the water so easily disturbs and terrifies me; to know there is such power outside our land is beyond my mind.

The beast heaves itself forward, shattering huge chunks of rotting ice in seconds. Anything with this strength, being so brash in its use, is not welcome. Though this thing is powerful, it is clumsy; such power needs to be used with caution. I know and confirm this within myself because I must wield great power one day, to guide our people, protect the ones I love, to protect Uumma.

Still studying the beast from a distance, I watch as Mirayualuk approaches it with caution and wild interest. Not even the children approach, too afraid this beast may swallow them whole. I share their fears. The elders scoff at Mirayualuk's brazen attitude, the women shame him with their scowls, the youth are confused. Seeing one of our own so absorbed in something so foreign makes me worry that his heart lies elsewhere.

The beast opens a part of itself onto the ice with a blast that would shatter ears. The air within me ejects, forced out by dread I have never felt before. My breath is struggling to keep pace with me as I run to my bow. My body is moving faster than I can think. I feel confident, knowing my instincts guide me. I turn back to see the eldest men herding everyone to their tents, not aware or not caring that Mirayualuk is close enough to talk to the beast.

Walking closer, careful, vigilant, ready, I watch as Mirayualuk talks to the hole in the beast. I hear footsteps behind me, the other elders readying their bows. Mirayualuk watches me as I approach; he is making many gestures to whatever is in the hole. I hear deep, hollow footsteps within the beast, becoming louder very quickly. What appears is a man, but he is so different. Skin like the snow, hair like a fire, clothes like rags. He is not of this land. He is not ready. This man will die here.

Upon seeing my bow, the man scurries behind the door, yelling at Mirayualuk in sounds that hardly carry beyond the small logs leading to the hole. With annoyance in his voice, Mirayualuk tells me that the man with the hair like fire brings gifts, in exchange for our things. I tell him I do not understand. It is not *our things*. It is everyone's, and no one's. We all share it. Mirayualuk says he knows this, but the man in the hole offers a way off this island, to a new land.

"You want to leave?" I say, confused by the thought. To leave everything, abandoning the things I have known since childhood, never seeing Uumma again. These thoughts confuse me. I feel shame for Mirayualuk.

"I want to see the world beyond this ocean. I want to see the place where these beasts are built."

I nod. The thought of leaving Uumma makes me want to see her, embrace her.

"Go, I will talk to the man. It is late." He is right. The eternal sun helps me sleep, somehow. The elders will decide on someone to watch the beast while the village rests. I return to my tent, wary that Mirayualuk is not who I thought he was.

I awake to shouting. Uumma is not here. Mirayualuk is not here. The beast is leaving. Eyelids, heavy. Mind, hot. Mirayualuk did this. He is dead. I need my bow. I need my *qusunngaq*, to keep warm. I need arrows. He is dead. I am running towards the beast, wearing only the bottoms of my *qusunngaq*. Near Uumma's tent, a pack of black and brown furs is stacked high. They took Uumma from me. They took her for furs. She is everything and she is gone. Mirayualuk will die.

My bow and arrows are floating ahead of me as I swim. My arms move in and out of the water, swiftly. I am watching the beast become larger, darker. Stabbing the beast with an arrow, my hands grasp tight, pulling myself up. My feet find logs to grip into—a hand grabs my arm, pulling me upward, onto the beast's back. I fall hard on my back, breath escaping. I turn to face the sky. A log comes down upon my face, a foot to my chest. Hate fills my lungs, my mouth. I scream at Mirayualuk. I scream for Uumma. I am beaten again. Darkness.

The moon attacks my eyes, making me see only a pale shade of white. A shove comes from my left, guiding me towards the glow. Glimpses of white and black enter my eyes, feebly trying to make sense of everything. Callused hands force me to somewhere cold, in the bright midnight. A mighty shove, a kick to the back of my ankle, and I am on my knees. My body is hot with pain and anger, but the air flows through me. Calming.

My eyes can see. They see Uumma. That is all they need to see. She is nearly naked in the *tunik's* rags, bruised everywhere.

No more hate for anyone. Only want to connect.

I crawl to her on my knees, happy to know she is still alive, still waiting. I rest my head on her belly. Soft. Comforting. I am home.

JORDAN CARPENTER, author of *Finding Home*, is a novice writer/university undergrad/lifeguard. He isn't sure why he writes but it's something he enjoys. He feels if he can make an audience feel what he does he has accomplished his work as a writer. Of Inuit heritage, Jordan hopes writing will lead him to a better understanding of his ancestry. *Finding Home* is his first published story.

Born a Girl

by Richard Van Camp

Steve nods as Dougie lifts me off the ground. I smell scalp, tar, heat. I huff and push all my air out until my lungs whistle and I get dizzy. They call this the Fainting Game, and I wish the sky would blow me in half as Dougie squeezes my ribs tight—so tight my face burns and balloons. Three pelicans soar above. As the rush comes, I wonder if they can see me back. Heat from my skull explodes and *there they are*: sparks of day fire. Dougie bear hugs me and holds me high—I hear a rib pop—and the next thing I know my ears are roarin', and I have a two-by-four. I'm in slow motion running and falling sideways as my head roars and everyone cheers, "Zombie!"

I see all the grade eights and nines flee, spilling over the fence and road in terror from me. Clarence has climbed to the top of a tree and Dougie is crying, holding his leg going, "Fuck you, Kevin!" and I wipe out slowwwwwwwwwwwwwwwwwwwly, drop the two-by-four and collapse sore-throated and body ringing. My body blurs of everything and I have nothing left of me.

After Steve lifts me, holds me, and walks me home he grins, "That was the best Zombie yet."

My eyes bulge out of their sockets and everybody looks so much younger with short hair, even the teachers, even the principal, and now the mayor and the chief of the Salt River First Nation and the president of the Métis Association, and now the chief of the Fitz Smith Band, and now our MLA, and we are waiting to hear about our MP, but his wife—I know for sure his wife cut her hair. What happened here was on CBC and it's spreading. Everyone's cut their hair because of what happened to Brian. My face goes numb when I think about it, so I don't.

Steve and Dougie are my disciples. Sometimes I sense that life is all a play. Like when I'm out of the room, everyone stops and waits for me to return. Like nobody's real. I think Steve and Dougie are real. I know for sure that Brian's real. I've never told anyone this but it's like I'm the last real person on earth, but I'm vanishing.

We watch *Freddy vs. Jason* for the hundredth time in the dark. Steve lies behind me, and I wonder if we're fags. I don't care. I think I'm dying faster than everybody because of Zombie. I accept it. Steve's a chronic shoplifter from the drugstore and today his underarms smell like mint. He reaches over me for a sip of water and I back into him as he does.

"Wait," I say. "Jason's afraid of water. What's Freddy afraid of again?"

He takes a sip. "Fuck, man. You always ask this." I shift my body closer as the mattress sinks. I bet if we were ever naked he'd go for it and maybe I'd let him.

"He's afraid of being forgotten." I close my eyes and try and remember this. Why can't I remember this?

"What do you think about when you go Zombie?" I'm blushing with how close we are. I can also smell the detergent his mom uses: lemon something. "Like, where do you go?"

"I don't know." He brushes my hip as he shifts, but I know. I think I know. I think of the disciple who does Brian's makeup in the handicapped washroom. Kelsey. The redhead. Pretty, blue-eyed and May Day princess Kelsey who always walks like she's just been gut punched. She must know we can all see her glow-in-the-dark scars on her wrists. How she must wince when the shower hits. I remember her when we were in kindergarten, how she used to stand alone under the fort and shiver, even when it was hot out. I'm going to try and tell her to stop being so scared of herself the next time I see her. I want to do that. I hope I remember to do that.

I could also fuck her for practice.

I also think about beating up Brian. I loved making him cry. I'd race after him when I saw him. "Makeup Warrior," I called him, and then I'd ask, "Why?" (punch) "Why?" (shove) "Why?" (kick) "Why?" (knee). I'd Sally Cow him so he couldn't use his arms and then Charlie Horse him so he'd push to the ground. "You fuckin' fag. Why?" He'd start to cry and I'd grin. I kept trying to knock him down with a punch to the temple or a knee to the chin but he'd tuck his head away. *Why?*

I feel Steve's breath against the back of my neck. I am the most ferocious Zombie in Fort Smith history, even though this town is just the illusion of life. We Zombie every chance we get. Sometimes we use hockey socks or bandanas by ourselves, but mostly we just choke, squeeze and huff each other, and this is why I'm dying faster than anyone. A month ago we licked frogs from the swamp. It was supposed to get us high but we both ended up throwing up behind the house all afternoon.

We also did that stupid thing where we taped golf balls over our eyes and turned the TV to snow and cranked it for half an hour because it's supposed to be the new séance. You're supposed to hear the dead. All I could do was sit there and start crying.

I feel like I'm running out of skin and my wrists are burning off.

I can tell Dougie totally fakes when it's his turn to Zombie, and Steve just sits there drooling through his hands. Nobody but me lifts the two-by-four to chase the crowd. The students wait for me to do it, and the teachers never catch on because they're all smoking off school property and texting their old ladies now that Smith got cell phones.

Fort Smith, NWT. Métis capital of the north. Home of the last legal hanging in Canada. Our dance hall is the Roaring Rapids Hall but it's also known as Moccasin Square Gardens because of all the fights. Dad says Smith is so tough even the rain here has knuckles. I've tried to think about Zombie, and I know it's about being held. I lean into Steve. I love it when he holds me. My body sings with his muscles and the smell of his hot scalp and his dad's cologne: a quiet fire of something pretty, something burning. I sniff it every time we're watching pornos at his house.

"Why?" I yelled at Brian as mascara ran down his face. "Why do you dress like a girl when you're a boy? Why?" I loved how his body twisted and gave under my punches. I'd drive his body with each upper cut, and I loved the sounds he made as he slumped into me. He was wearing a skirt and heels. "Why? Why the fuck are you like this?"

But this is not the worst I've done to him.

Last night, me and Steve were walking by the college. I flushed the toilet downstairs and snuck out while the sound was loud and there was Steve with his bike and mine. He knows my combo. We rode out together and the town was ours. We rode up to the Welfare Centre and to Frontier Village and even to both trailer courts and then by the college residences. There, we passed by a volleyball team. Girls. Diamond Jenness hoodies. Hay River girls.

"Heyyyyyyyyyy," one with huge glasses on said as we drove by.

Steve hit the brakes. "Helloooooooooooo." I wanted to keep going but they surrounded us.

"Got a mickey?" one of them asked.

"No," Steve said.

"Well, we do." Big Glasses said and the rest laughed. "Wanna party with us?"

"Sure," Steve said. He gave me a look like we'd struck gold. I wanted to go home. Before I knew it, we stashed our bikes and snuck in through the first floor windows at the college residence.

"Shhh," Big Glasses said. "Our coach has a black belt. We can't wake him."

Next thing you know we're sitting on a bed and we're surrounded by seven girls. Five of which are considerable. Two are mugwumps. They're older than us and Steve passed me a bottle as we made introductions. I wrinkled my nose and forgot everyone's names.

Steve took two swigs in a row. I hate alcohol and he knows not to offer.

"So what do you two do for fun in Fart Sniff?" one of the girls asks. She has a big nose and braces.

Steve looks to me. "We play Zombie."

"Zombie?" Big Glasses asks. She has a nice body.

"Zombie," Steve says. "Here, we'll show you," and he stands. I know he wants to do it to me, but I say no. I flick my wrist and that's our sign for *no, this is ours. Why share it?* He glances at me and looks back at the girls.

"We're waiting," one says. "Don't be cheap. You two are ambassadors for Fort Smurf."

I wanted the one with cinnamon eyes. She must have been Gwichi'in. She had the same body as the one I saw in my first porno, so I know what she'd look like taking it hard standing looking down, her hands reaching for whatever she could as her tits slapped together. I'd like to stand close to her naked and feel her heat all over my face. I bet she'd look great under the red heat lamp in Steve's dad's sauna. I think I could tell her the truth as I finger her slowly: *I broke something. I did. I fucking hate myself for what I did to Brian. I do. Forgive me, okay?* Maybe I could do this with Kelsey.

"Take it easy," Steve says. "You're from Gay River."

"At least we don't half kill transsexuals," Big Glasses says. The girls all go, "Ooooooh" and Steve looks at me and I blush and look down. I am suddenly ashamed. *We went too far. Why?*

"Why didn't you cut your hair?" one girl asks. "All the guys in Hay River did."

"And half the girls," another joins.

"I'm thinking about it," Steve says and this surprises me. *Really?* My eyes ask him but he's not looking at me anymore.

"Let's play truth or dare," one girl says. A brunette with a sharp nose.

"Uh oh," Big Glasses says. "Here comes the Sexpert."

Steve and I glance at each other.

"How do you jack off?" she asks and points at me. "You first. Then we'll all go."

Two of the girls bury their hands in their faces and start kicking the bed giggling and the others go, "Shh. Shh. Don't wake the coach." I suddenly love being here. I can smell perfume wafting from them and I see all their suitcases. And then I see her. There's a girl standing in the corner of a large closet with her nose in the corner. She is wearing her bra—pink and small—backwards on the outside of her shirt. She has two bandaids on the back of the heels of her bare feet.

"Never mind her," Big Nose says. "Rebecca's being punished."

"Twat!" one of the girls whispers and they all laugh.

Steve gives me a look like we're in over our heads.

"I want to know," she says. "Sorry. We all want to know."

"Yeah," the girls all say. "How? How? Tell us."

Steve looks at me absolutely horrified. "Take it fuckin' easy. I'm not going to tell you."

"Okay, loser," one of the girls says. "I have a question about the gay boy."

Steve and I look at her.

"Rebecca's cousin says that police are investigating his father for holding him down and cutting off his hair."

Steve and I look at each other. "What?"

She nods. "Did his dad cut off his hair and then tie him up with his own clothes?"

"Where did you hear this?" I ask.

"It's on the news. We heard it on the way in."

"His dad didn't cut off his hair," Rebecca says softly.

"Shut it!" Big Nose says. "Speak ONLY when you are being spoken to or we'll make you do a lot more than you're already going to." Rebecca nods. I'd love to see her face. Steve and I look at each other. So that's why he had short hair. *His dad?*

"Yeah," Lip Ring says, "my cousin said Brian's dad had just received a call from a parent saying, 'Keep your *It* away from my kids.' Apparently, his folks didn't know he was leaving the house a boy and showing up to class a girl."

"How could you not know that?" Steve asks.

"So what was with the honey?" the Boss asks. "His dad covered him with honey?"

"No," Lip Ring says. "His gran needed honey for some bannock and he had, like, four huge bottles."

"So, his dad tied him to a tree and poured four bottles of honey all over him while he was upside down?"

Breath spins in my throat as my face goes numb. I see sparks without any help from anyone as my stomach sinks. *So that's why he didn't run or fight back.* It must have been the day after. On the way to his grandma's. Where we cut him off.

"Anyhow," one of the girls says, "we're thinking of ditching practice tomorrow to welcome him back to school."

"What do you mean?"

"He's out of the hospital tonight," the leader says. And she's watching us. She's onto us.

I glare at Steve. He's looking at his fingers. My face is burning. There goes my wrists.

"I'm bored," one of the girls says. "What is this Zombie?"

Steve gives me a dirty look and kicks off his dad's cowboy boot and pulls off his hockey sock and wraps it around his neck and pulls as he starts to huff. "I'll show you."

"No, wait. Steve—" I say because this is getting good. I need to know more about Brian.

Steve wraps his hockey sock around his neck so tight his neck veins bulge like suffocating earthworms. He holds it and pulls harder. He starts to buck and twitch and the girls all back away from him before he shoots back and flies off the bed smacking his skull on the heater. A jet of blood sprays the wall and the girls scream. Steve starts to seizure and the girls all race off out of the room to get their coach. The room is a blur of crazy panic. The girl in the corner turns to look at me and all I see in her eyes is hate. I grab Steve and drag him. He makes the noises Johnny Knoxville made when Butterbean knocked him out with one punch in *Jackass*: "Gnnnhhh Gnnnuuuuhhhhhh."

"It was you, wasn't it?" the girl in the corner asks. "You poured the honey over him, right?" I glance at her. WHORE and CUNT are written over her entire face in the shape of the cross. "I can hear it in your voice." Her eyes are pure white. Is she blind?

Steve kicks and snorts in my arms as I heave and push him through the window while the girls run for their black belt coach. Steve lands on his neck on the pavement under the window and I drag him around the corner and hide behind the dumpster as he drools and sputters all over himself and there's his bare foot all dusty now and his big toe nail's snapped up and blue. I drag him over the pavement and lie down in the bush as the outside lights of the residence come on.

We cornered Brian in the bush. On his way home. He was carrying groceries from the Northern. It was honey. Four of the biggest bottles ever. I was with Steve. "Cut your hair, hey, you little fag?"

It was true. Short hair only accentuated his features even more. His big eyes. His earrings. He was gorgeous.

One look said it all. He looked down in complete surrender. He was dressed as a boy this time but I could see his earrings. We surrounded him. Started pushing him. "Why?" I'd push him over and over. "Why?" He was wearing lipstick and eye shadow.

"Why?"

"Yeah," Steve said and kicked him hard in the back. "Why?"

"Don't," I wanted to say. I'd never beaten Brian up with anyone else. I didn't like it. With Brian, I was the cat and he was the mouse. I loved making him cry. He was so fucking unreal it gave me pleasure hitting him, downing him. I pulled his pants off and was tempted to pull off his gonch but thought *no. Too much.* Steve ripped his shirt off his body and stomped him into the earth so hard a branch underneath him snapped. I winced.

We ended tying Brian up upside down with his clothes to a tree. It was Steve's idea to pour the honey all over his legs, up his shorts, down his legs and leave him. I got so into it I didn't know. But the thing is he didn't scream. He didn't. Brian just looked away as we beat him. As I punched him so hard I connected with bone. I heard a pop. I can still hear the breath leaving his body as Steve stomped him in the chest. I can still hear that SNAP!

I lie down behind Steve and pull him close. He's out cold now, quiet.

I think I poured the honey all over Brian, but I want to say it was Steve. Upside down. Brian looking away, crying quietly but no tears, honey searching his body. He'd shaved his legs. I felt the stubble when I held him and we used his shirt and jacket as rope.

I had no fucking idea honey would pool towards his mouth. I didn't know the honey'd go inside. I had no idea. Upside down and alone. In the bush, a mile from his home. He must have been so scared, and I did this to him. We did but it was mostly me.

Mostly me.

An hour later at the landslide, that's when I heard the ambulance. We were smoking. I knew it was for him.

I was secretly worried when we walked away. I thought he'd get down, wiggle his way out. I had no idea the honey would hunt for his mouth and nose, that he'd drown that way. That no matter how much he panicked and shook his head back and forth, the honey would pool to find the inside of his nostrils, mouth, eyes, ears.

So why the fuck didn't he run? I wondered. *Why didn't he struggle?*

We'd crucified him upside down with honey and that was the night after—when I dare myself to think about it—that was the night after his father held him down and cut off all his hair.

Keep your "It" away from my kid.

Brian didn't run because his heart was broken. What did he have left? We were his final humiliation.

It was Mr. Harris who found him. Walking his dog. It was Mr. Harris who pulled him down and scooped the honey out of his throat, his nose. His wife is a nurse. Mr. Harris volunteers for the ambulance. His wife used her mouth to suck the honey out of his nose. They say his lips were blue. Brian's eyes were fused shut. He was deaf. The honey was swelling inside his skull.

He must have wanted to die. As we worked him over with kicks and punches, as we hung him upside down and tied him up, he looked away because he had no tears left.

As the coach comes running outside holding the longest flashlight in human history, I pull Steve deeper into shadows. I go, "Shhhhhhh," "Shhh," "Shh." I hold him and he sags into me. I get a waft of warm air off his body and smell his pit-stick: *cinnamon*.

That image of Brian there, all crucified upside down, is inside me. All of me. Behind my eyelids, souring my blood. "We went too far," I finally say.

Steve comes to and asks, "Where's my boot?"

"You lost it."

"What?"

I point with my chin towards the residence. "It's in there."

"Go get it," he says and it's his tone that gets me.

"You, you fuckin' asshole."

He sits up. "What?"

"You go get it, you fuckin' fag," I finally say.

He turns to me and blinks wide. "What did you call me?"

I back away from him as he rises. "You heard me."

He struggles to stand. "Did you just call me a fag?"

I plant my feet. "Yup."

"Fuck you," he says and pushes me.

"You know you want to fuck me and that'll never happen so you fuckin' go get your dumb boot."

The first punch slams my bottom tooth half through my top lip. I never saw that coming. I push my full weight into Steve but I let him snap my body and head with kicks, knees and punches. He slaps my ear and I feel the pop of pure white pain behind my eyes and that's when I pretend to be Brian. When Steve slows, I call him a fag over and over and he backs up before coming back with kicks, hammer fists and knees. He gets to finally use every move he's ever wanted—even with only one boot on.

"If you ever tell," he hisses, "I'll kill you. I swear to fuckin' God I will."

I end up on the ground with my head roaring, ear hot and ringing, blowing bubbles with my own blood. I think of Brian tied upside down with honey reaching for his mouth. "No problem, fag."

I don't know what he did next but I heard a wet crunch and came to later with him gone. I look up into the eyes of the night and start sucking for breath. Glass is through my lung. That has to be a rib. That's when I started to cry. "I'm sorry," I kept saying over and over. "I'm so fucking sorry."

Today it's quarter to nine. Brian always arrives at quarter to nine. It's his first day back. He comes in and he is bald. He must have shaved it all off. Or maybe the nurses. Or his mom. I have a fat lip and when I breathe too deep, there's something like shards of window glass against my right lung. I'm leaning against the wall with my eye swollen shut.

I look like shit and have been squeezing my fat lip over and over until what is left—after the blood—is water. I lap it as I squeeze and it seeps into me. All of me.

And there he is … Brian's wearing lipstick this morning. He is so beautiful. Even more beautiful than ever. Even with a black eye and a limp. Is it his doe eyes, his sharp nose, or how tiny he is?

I look around and everyone has cut their hair. As Brian walks towards the foyer, we all stand. He stops and looks around and sees all the students and teachers have cut their hair off.

Steve's not here. The pigs were at his house this morning. I saw the paddy wagon and turned around.

Coming Home

Why? I ask myself. I would always ask Brian that, but there's no way he could answer. He could never have known what I was really asking him. I cut all my hair off this morning. I want him to see me like this. I need him to see me like this. There's Kelsey. She's shaved all her red hair off and looks so tiny, like a bird falling to her death. She's beside him now. She's crying, touching his eye. And then I see his arms: they're purple—his wrists, too. Rope burns. From what we did. My legs go dead when I realize this, and there's the police. The paddy wagon pulls right up to the foyer. Shit! I can almost see Steve in the back seat. I wonder if he's cut his hair. I bet you a million dollars he's looking at his fingers.

And there's the volleyball team from last night. Big Nose, Big Glasses—all of them—simply all of them—have cut their hair short. The man beside Big Nose looks in my direction and he looks tough. Mean. He starts to make his way towards me the exact moment I see two RCMP members come through the door. They spot me.

I have seconds left. I have to move fast. I look at Brian and start clapping first. Brian looks at me. For a second, he is confused. He squints—when he focuses and sees it's me. I pray he sees my haircut. I did it last night as soon as I got home. Dad was waiting. He was like, "Kevin, fuck sakes anyways. I don't want you drunk driving with my truck."

I chopped my hair off by myself and didn't even care how I looked. "I'll stop when you stop," I called even though it was Steve. My hair feathered and twirled into the sink.

I want to sink into hot knives for what I've done to Brian who looks my way as the RCMP and the coach with the black belt approach and corral me. I'm all out of time. I broke something beautiful and hate myself for it. I am clapping as loud as I can before the school catches on. As Brian looks my way, I can tell he is confused, but he is thinking. He is thinking about when I last looked into his eyes as I punched and swung and punched him again and again. I think he read my mind. As hard as I swung and as hard as

I hit he must have seen it in my eyes: the question and the answer to my *Why?*

Why, Brian? Why the fuck are you so beautiful, and why have I always wanted you so much?

RICHARD VAN CAMP, author of *Born a Girl*, is a proud member of the Tlicho Dene from Fort Smith, NWT. His novel, *The Lesser Blessed*, is now a movie with First Generation Films starring Benjamin Bratt, Kiowa Gordon, Chloe Rose and Fort Smith's very own Joel Evans. His new short story collection, *Godless but Loyal to Heaven*, is out with Enfield & Wizenty, and his new baby book, *Little You*, will appear in 2013 with Orca Book Publishers. Richard writes and publishes in every genre.

Angatkuq

by Marcus Jackson

Jack's body was still rolling with the breath of the ocean and he could feel thunder in his teeth every time he was lucid. His dreams were crowded with images of ice, pulsating whitecaps, arthritic fists, freezing rain and snow—so much snow. Voices inside his head shouted death threats, begged, whispered prayers and wept. One voice was louder than all the others and persistent as the gulls that followed the tiny boat. That voice belonged to his crazy father, whose voice was like an angry stammering toddler. The bodies of his shipmates blackened and melted around him while the stench of scurvy-rotted teeth and shit nauseated even his memory. He wasn't sure he had yet survived, but secretly Jack prayed he was alone.

The first time he could open his eyes it was dark. A rock seemed to burn next to the bed. A strange-smelling smoke filled his nostrils, burning the backs of his eyeballs. Jack was covered with the fur skin of an animal that, by the wet meaty smell of it, hadn't been dead very long. His skin felt tight and as fragile as fresh vellum; his fat dry tongue no longer fit inside his mouth. His water-logged delirium made him feel as if he were falling. He turned toward a figure kneeling beside him who nodded and grunted for him to drink from a stone saucer. The liquid was salty and oily, warm lumps coagulated beneath the surface. He tried not to choke as it slid down his throat. A cube of thick fatty meat was placed between his lips and the figure nodded again, encouraging him to eat. It was disgusting but his stomach was not dissuaded. He fell into dream once again, the blubber only half-chewed in his open mouth.

Often Jack couldn't tell if he was awake or asleep or floating someplace on a raft between the two worlds. He dreamt of swimming under green ice, catching fish between his teeth, and sliding along snow on his belly. The howling and yipping of wolves was surely inside his head but he startled when a pack of hundreds brushed past his legs as he ran. And there were lights. Ribbons of pink and green that danced across the sky, magic of a kind only the Vikings might have known. The flickering glow illuminated the sky above the carcass of a wide-horned beast. Jack feasted upon its wet flesh beside a giant silver bear and a hideous mermaid. The bear's eyes were as black as the night sky and his fur so soft, so fine, so white Jack could have sworn it was made of stars. The mermaid's voluptuous brown breasts spilled over her spotted fleshy torso and when she laughed the whole earth seemed to shake. He drank blood from the moon out of a cup made of twisted bone. His strange dreams carried on for days. Underneath it all was a quiet vibration that seemed to come from under the ground.

The caretaker washed Jack's face and fed him solid food. He guessed it was some kind of fish wrapped in a thick wet leaf. It tasted not too bad. The pasty grey food he'd been eating till now had finally given him enough strength to prop himself up in bed and hold a cup of hot tea-like liquid. She slathered him in a thick yellow jelly that smelled like the inside of his boots. He could hear her singing and sometimes humming while she sewed and chewed at bits of leather. She held some sort of dried meat for him and smiled.

More time passed before he felt strong enough to be guided out of the dark room by his nurse; she was stronger than he imagined. When his eyes finally adjusted to the light, the land that lay before him was like nothing he had ever seen in his sixteen years. The land stretched as far as he could see—not a single building or sign of civilization. The earth undulated in ripples and parts of it seemed to be alive and moving. The thrumming sound was there like the endless thunder in his dreams only quieter and he felt the constant vibration beneath his feet.

The scent of vegetation and brine drifted on the cold breeze. His skin erupted in goose flesh and a shiver ran through his body. Again he felt as if his bones had been frozen. The woman gripped him tighter to keep him from falling. It was then he realized that this was not a woman at all but a sturdy little man with a very pretty face. Jack tried to speak but the ragged whisper passed over his tongue and tangled itself between his teeth before he could form it into words. The stranger shook his head and mumbled something, pointing at the horizon. Jack scanned the valley and watched, as the dark rippling form he thought was a hill became a giant swarm of animals. He couldn't make out individuals only a mass of tiny bodies swarming along the edge of a valley headed towards their destination with single-minded determination. The man beside him made a noise in his throat and began speaking in a language Jack could only describe as a stutter.

The ocean crossing eroded Jack's body, leaving a darker, harder fossil of his former self. His fingers and toes had been gnawed by frost over the course of the winter in much the same way his father's mind had been eaten by madness. The crew was hungry and weathered from an eternally desperate winter trapped in the ice. Eventually they threw father, son, and a handful of loyalists off the ship, turned it east, and headed back to England, leaving the tiny group stranded with a lunatic at the helm.

The eight of them drifted for weeks while his father grew greedy for imagined glory. William and Thomas died of despair and frustration, Jack was sure. Philip and Edward, who had abandoned the ship and crew with only their loyalty to a madman to feed them, perished quietly of starvation before the storm even hit. Francisco, Herman, and Jack's own father undoubtedly drowned; their bodies likely washed up on a rocky shore and were feasted upon by scavengers. How Jack had survived when he'd never learned to swim was a mystery.

Dreams entered him in the cover of dark but now they were brash and possessed him at will, even in the middle of the day. Fish with horns, hulking hairless dogs, black foxes with silver eyes, a thousand talking black birds and a giant flying eyeball swirled around in his head. He wanted to draw. He somehow conveyed to the little man what he wanted and with a crude bone stylus on a long narrow piece of skin, he made pictures of his dreams from animal blood. The pictures on the skin grew more elaborate as he tried to re-create the dreams as accurately as his limited artistic skills would allow.

His companion in the darkness sang quietly while he sewed, brought food as foreign to Jack's tongue as the language was to his ears. His companion took him on longer and longer walks every day and he felt urgency in the little man's voice as the wind got colder. Jack realized there was another journey for him on the horizon....

After a particularly long bout of sleep the little man set a pair of boots down in front of Jack and motioned him to put them on. The thin red scar tissue on his heels had just recently formed and his toes were still tender but the boots felt like brand new feet. The little man pulled a heavy skin jacket over Jack's head and took his hand. The man looked around the little room for a moment as if making sure there was nothing he was forgetting and they headed out into the sunset toward the sound of the thunder. They walked for what seemed like hours but as the sun never seemed to set it was difficult for Jack to tell how long they had been walking. He was pleasantly surprised at his endurance: the rhythm of the vibration kept him moving.

His mind found its own way into the dreamland more and more, as if the resonance of the vibration had unlocked a door between two worlds. Jack seemed to be able to see things he could not explain but his waking dream images were different from those he saw in his sleep. As the thunder got louder the images became clearer. He saw another little man with a belt made of skin and covered in blood. Through the star-speckled darkness he could see cold figures falling out of the sky and writhing out of the sea. There were buildings made of secrets, boats made of bones and skin, packs of singing dogs, purple velvet pouches filled with teeth, yellow rocks splattered with blood, deep canyons clawed into the land, burning steeples, weeping eagles, and a boy with dark hair and blue eyes wearing a skin belt covered in drawings....

Coming Home

Jack nearly crashed into the back of his companion, unsure if he had been sleepwalking. The little man pointed to a bump on the horizon and made a noise. Jack looked at him and smiled. He had no idea what else to do. The little man smiled back and Jack was struck with a sorrow so profound he could not understand it. The images flooded back and this little man was in all of them somehow. He felt a vibration blossom in his chest as if suddenly a hundred humming birds filled his heart. Jack had no idea where the two of them were headed or where they would be when they finally arrived. He just let his feet carry him across the earth as he wept quietly, following the little man who was humming a song Jack had heard over and over in his dreams.

MARCUS JACKSON, author of *Angatkuq*, is an artist and writer living in Yellowknife with his three cats. He participated in (and finished) the 2011 NaNoWriMo challenge and wrote his first novel in just thirty days! He is now editing said novel and planning another. Marcus writes two blogs on an irregular basis and occasionally reads the dictionary for fun. He studied writing at the University of Calgary and the fine art of print media at Alberta College of Art and Design. *Angatkuq* is Marcus's first published work.

Celia's Inner Anorexic

by Annelies Pool

Celia was in Shopper's Drug Mart when Bryan caught her reading a sleazy tabloid. She hadn't intended to pick up the *Women's Universe* but she had a cold and her head was stuffed like her underwear drawer. She felt fat, and at work she'd struck the wrong key and sent her report into virtual la-la land, and ... in short, her defenses were down so that when she walked past the magazine rack, the headline snaked out and vibrated in front of her eyes.

1,359-POUND WOMAN TRAPPED IN ROOM!

My God! Could it be true? With a guilty glance down the aisle, Celia picked it up and began to read.

The woman was addicted to tortieres. She wrote poetry about flakey crusts and rhapsodized about spiced ground meat. The woman had eaten so many of the meat pies that now she couldn't get through her front door, and had to have them delivered from a deli down the street. Her daughter was frantic, had begged her mother to stop....

Celia read with that horror-movie fascination where you don't really want to watch but you can't stop. That's when Bryan came up behind her, cradled her hips and crooned in her ear, "still reading the literary stuff, hey?"

Celia's face blazed fluorescent as a jumble of images sped through her mind. Bryan's naked back splotched with pink liquid. A bouquet of yellow flowers. The Mackenzie Valley Pipeline Inquiry. She wished she could transform *Women's Universe* into a copy of *Harper's*. She wanted to sink through the floor, then she wanted to punch him.

Crushing the tabloid against her chest, she whipped around. "W-what are you doing in Yellowknife?"

Bryan raised his hands "Whoa!" he said.

"You're not supposed to be here!"

"Settle down," he said. "School's out. I'm back for the summer."

"Oh." He slid his eyes over her boobs and down her belly and laughed in that lazy, paddling-down-the-river way that had always gone straight to Celia's groin.

"Hey," he grinned. "You're looking ample." Celia looked down, then snapped her head up and glared.

"Ample? What's that supposed to mean?"

"Celia, I...."

She didn't wait for an answer. Still clutching the tabloid, Celia stormed out of the store, not realizing until she was out on the street that she hadn't paid for it. She fumed that Bryan had turned her into a shoplifter, then dithered between the urge to go back in and pay, and the terror of seeing him again. At the same time, she wished he had come after her and she hated herself for wanting him to. She was a mess, a stuffed-up, eye-watering mess.

Fishing a bedraggled tissue out of her pocket, Celia blew her nose and looked around. The temperature had risen to five above and melting snow dripped from the roof of the Panda Mall. People walked down the street with open coats. Fat ravens feasted on a carton of fries beside a pickup truck that sported a "fish for sale" sign.

Her nostrils temporarily clear, Celia took a deep yoga breath to centre herself. The air was soft and laced with the smell of deep-fried chicken from the KFC outlet down the street. Celia was struck by a longing for a piece of crunchy, salty chicken. She wanted to sink her teeth into a drumstick. She wanted to feel rivulets of grease slide down her chin.

Twenty minutes later, Celia arrived home with a box of chicken and the *Women's Universe* tucked under her arm. Her kitchen was bright and familiar. The sun shone through the window and lit the avocado-green fridge, highlighting a photo of a young woman on a staircase, leaning against a wrought-iron railing. The picture was surrounded by fridge magnets. Celia dumped the chicken and tabloid on the table, heaved her coat onto a chair and kicked off the Birkenstocks that she put on every year as soon as the temperature rose above freezing. She wiped her nose and went into the bedroom, unfastening her wraparound dress so that it slid down her body and puddled on the floor. She unhooked her bra and sighed at the release. Then she found her favourite flannel nightgown and pulled it over her head.

Back in the kitchen, Celia raided the cupboards and unearthed bags of red licorice and Oreo cookies, a jar of honey and a nearly-full bottle of brandy. She made tea and put everything on a giant serving tray that she carried into the bedroom and balanced on the unused side of the bed. She crawled under the covers, propped herself up with pillows and made herself a potion of tea, honey and brandy. The liquor's warmth spread through her chest. Celia chose a drumstick and sucked the meat off the bone, imagining herself at the court of Henry VIII in Tudor England. She threw the bone on the floor, then ripped the licorice bag open with her teeth and hosed out a length.

The scene with Bryan replayed in her mind. Ample, he'd called her. What *was* that supposed to mean?

Celia had fallen for Bryan by mistake. She had met him the summer before at a solstice party, a sexy guy with a ponytail and tight jeans leaning against the refrigerator with the relaxed air of a *dude*. He had fathomless brown eyes, a diamond stud in one ear and a tattoo of a wolf on his right bicep. He looked at her with that sensuality that some young men carry for older women. Celia offered him a glass of wine.

They found a free corner in the living room and sat on the floor cross-legged and facing each other. Bryan said he had come to Yellowknife for the summer to research his thesis on the Berger Inquiry into the Mackenzie Valley pipeline, from back in the seventies. That was when Celia realized she had found her soulmate.

Six months earlier, Celia had moved to Yellowknife from Ontario to take a government job. On her first day at work, she had found a file of clippings about the inquiry stuck behind a drawer of her desk. The story catapulted her into another world. Celia's heart melted as she read about the Dene, getting up to the mike, one after another in all the little Mackenzie Valley communities, to testify to the importance of their land. When she read that they had succeeded in stopping the pipeline, she wanted to stand up and cheer. After that, she spent hours in the territorial archives doing research into the inquiry. Celia was now thinking about writing a book.

"It was all about empowerment," she enthused, leaning forward and gripping Bryan's arm. "They took on big business, and won. The first Aboriginal people in Canada to do anything like it!"

"Yes, it was huge!" said Bryan.

He reached over and tucked a strand of Celia's hair behind her ear. "I love your passion," he crooned.

Celia finished her tea, then took a slug of brandy straight out of the bottle. She picked the skin off a chicken breast, wrapped it around a licorice stick and bit into it. The combination was interesting: spice, sweet and grease all in one.

Celia and Bryan talked until they were the last ones at the party. Bryan loved Tolstoy's *Anna Karenina* as much as Celia did. They both admired Gandhi and thought the world would be a better place if people would only stop killing each other and treat others with respect, no matter the colour of their skin. At the end of the night, Bryan kissed her until her womb lurched. Then with a little boy look in his face, he asked her to take him home with her. It seemed to Celia that everything in her life had served to bring her to this moment with this man.

But he was so young.

He was only twenty-seven and at forty-six that made Celia old enough to be his mother.

She thought it might be okay for just one night.

Celia soothed her throat with another concoction of tea, brandy and honey, then reached into the Oreo bag, took out a cookie, split it in half and teased the white filling with her tongue.

The minute the door closed behind them, Celia and Bryan came together like magnets, kissing, touching, fondling and fumbling with hooks and zippers until their clothes were strewn across the living room.

Bryan was the kind of guy for whom sex was an athletic event. He was young and he had staying power. They did it sitting up, lying down, backwards, frontwards, sideways, her on top, him on top, legs open, legs closed, ankles up, ankles down. Him at her from behind while she leaned over the kitchen sink and pretended to wave at the neighbours. Her climbing him like a tree while he was propped up against the wall.

It was a bit like a three-ring circus. Celia was grateful for her yoga classes.

Celia washed the Oreo down with brandy and looked at the shelves against the bedroom wall. Books were piled two, three deep and reflected in her three-way mirror, making the room look like a big sloppy library. She and Bryan had been in the habit of reading to each other and discussing what they'd read, before love-making and after love-making. Sometimes even during.

Celia scrabbled for another piece of chicken, took a drink and flipped through the pages of *Women's Universe*. FIND THE TRUE THIN YOU, a headline bellowed from page five. Under it were "before" pictures of fleshy women in sweat pants, and "after" photos of the same women, skinny in bikinis. Celia liked the "before" shots better, and wondered why everybody had to be anorexic these days, why boobs had to be like raisins on pancakes and bellies concave. Bryan had called her his beautiful Rubens. He'd always said he liked her full breasts and the curve of her belly.

So what *did* he mean when he called her ample?

The morning after their first time, Celia told Bryan that it had been a magic night but that she was too old for him and they should never do it again. They agreed to be friends. That evening Bryan came over to show his new friend his thesis on the Mackenzie Valley Pipeline Inquiry. Within minutes they were rolling on Celia's bed and Bryan was sliding her panties down her thighs, while the thesis lay discarded on the floor. He rarely went home after that and they sunk into a private world of love, books and the Mackenzie Valley Pipeline Inquiry.

A part of Celia was shocked to find herself having an affair with such a young man and she often encouraged Bryan to find a woman closer to his own age. On another level, she became convinced that the age gap was not significant.

In late August, the day before Bryan was due to return to school in Edmonton, Celia had a business trip to Inuvik. Bryan took her to the airport, but left after a quick good-bye. As Celia watched his cab turn the corner, she felt insubstantial, as though a wind might blow her away at any moment. The feeling stayed with her and it was hard to pay attention at her meetings in Inuvik. She didn't feel the weight of herself again until the conference was unexpectedly cancelled late that afternoon.

After a night of restless dreams about Bryan, Celia arrived back in Yellowknife early the next day. She decided to surprise him and cabbed straight to his apartment, stopping on the way to get his favourite breakfast: a strawberry smoothie and cranberry-oatmeal muffins.

The door was unlocked. When Celia stepped inside, she was startled by a rhythmic banging, coming from the bedroom. A woman's voice cried "Yes! Yes! Yes!" Celia stormed across the living room to the open bedroom door and saw Bryan's butt pumping between a pair of young-looking thighs. Hurt, then rage, tore through her. The smoothie flew from her hand, shot through the air and crashed on Bryan's shoulder, splattering pink all over his back.

"What the hell?" said Bryan, craning his neck.

Celia dropped the bag of muffins and ran out of the apartment, down the hallway and out of the building, not stopping until she was several blocks away. Somehow she made it through her workday. That evening, she came home to a bright and lonely bouquet of daffodils in a glass on the kitchen table. Beside it was a plate of cranberry muffins. They were accompanied by a card that said:

Thanks for a wonderful summer. You are a great lady.
I will never forget you,
Bryan.
PS: Sorry about this morning. You know, timing?

Celia sank into a chair. She had always known something like this would happen. But she hadn't expected it would hurt this much. She ate the muffins.

Celia blew her nose again. So what did ample mean, anyway? Buxom? Portly? Generously endowed? Or maybe just fat?

She sighed and picked up the weight-loss article:

Deep inside each of us lives a slender, sultry woman. But we'll never find her as long as we think of ourselves as fat and ugly. Studies have shown that we can never hate ourselves into change. Only love can do that. Find the true thin inner you, by learning to love yourself the way you are.

Arm yourself with a notebook and pen. Then follow these easy steps, and watch the pounds melt away:

1. Remove your clothes, and sit in front of a full-length mirror.
2. Write a love letter to the part of your body you hate the most.
3. Repeat every day for three weeks.

Celia snorted, threw the tabloid on the floor and took another drink of brandy. She reached into the chicken box but only bones were left. Ample. The word beat in her mind like a morning-after headache. She took another drink, then said out loud, "maybe it's time to find my inner anorexic."

Celia turned up the heat, slipped the bolt on the door and took the phone off the hook. She got a pen and steno pad and dragged a chair from the kitchen to a spot directly in front of the large bedroom mirror. She removed her nightgown, sat down, blew her nose and looked at her reflection. She had a perfect view, from every angle, of just exactly how large her hips really were.

Dear Hips, she wrote.

Your great, gargantuan curves...

Celia put down her pen and thought about how Bryan used to lie on the bed, glorious in his nudity. She could never be that comfortable naked. No matter how he flattered her, Celia had always worn a diaphanous robe when they weren't under the covers or in the heat of the moment.

She looked back at the mirror. Her breasts had started to capitulate to the force of gravity. She sat up straight, held her breath, stuck out her chest and for a moment they look high and firm like they once were. But when she slumped back in the chair, her boobs slumped with her. Her eyes travelled down to her hips. Oh those hips....

Dear Hips,

Celia stopped. She didn't know if she really had anything to say to her hips. She took another slug of brandy and imagined herself a Victorian poetess writing to an illicit lover.

Dear Hips,
You, with your great, gelatinous plains of white, are the fortress guarding my channel into the mystery of womankind. Your ample expanse has been the inspiration of poets and artists throughout the ages. You have birthed nations....

Celia giggled and took another slug of brandy.

Dear Hips,
    You are supple, soft and strong. Your mammoth handfuls of flesh are the stuff of dreams. You are a temple of fertility.
    I love you. I love your rich, rolling, rollicking flesh. I love your winking dimples of cellulite. I love your over-stuffed, over-amplified, over-asserted, over-dramatic, over-equipped, over-achieving, over-whelming, over-spilling, over-abundance...."

Celia paused. Did she really want to love her hips? She usually fed what she loved. If she loved her hips too much, they would become so big, she wouldn't be able to get through the door. Just like the woman in the story. Her hips were like bag ladies. She wanted to be nice to them in a do-gooding, there-for-the-grace-of-God-go-I sort of way but she didn't want to be caught sitting in front of the post office with them.

Celia took another slurp of brandy.

"You're looking ample," Bryan had said. "Ample."

Dear Hips,
You are amply amplified in your amplitude.

Celia put down her pen and let the pad slide off her lap to the floor. The truth was that she didn't know what to do. She didn't know what to do about Bryan. She didn't know what to do about her life. She didn't know what to do about anything.

Celia looked at herself again. For the first time it sunk in that she was now well into middle-age. She was forty-seven years old, and her body had been alive for every minute of those forty-seven years. It had given her both pleasure and pain. She looked at the bumps, and the lumps, and the sags, and the dimples, until finally her eyes rested on the ladders of stretch marks on her belly.

Tricia, she whispered. She took another sip of brandy and back-handed the tear making its way down her cheek.

Tricia.

Celia felt again the haunting loneliness that had settled on her shoulders when she had watched Trish and Paul drive off in the cab to the airport the day they had married. She'd been happy for Trish, happy about the wedding, happy that Trish got to live in France. What mother wouldn't be? But… but….

Celia rose from her chair, walked into the kitchen and stopped in front of the picture on her refrigerator: Trish, fresh-faced and happy on the steps of her Paris walk-up. The photo had been taken on Trish's birthday in March. She was twenty-eight, the same age as Bryan. In the year and half since she had been married, Trish had sent her mom a ceramic fridge magnet every time she had a new adventure. Now Celia's fridge was covered with a tiny Paris. There was the Moulin Rouge, the Louvre, a sidewalk café, a phone booth by the Seine….

Celia plucked a miniature of Paris rooftops and held it up to the light so she could see the subtle glistening of raindrops, painted on the ceramic roofs. It was the first magnet Trish had given her and remained Celia's favourite. Trish had sent it with a sketch of two women, one young and one old, walking arm in arm down a Paris street in the European fashion. "That's you and me, Mom," she had written. "That's you and me."

Celia gently placed the magnet back in its spot beside the Ménagerie du Jardin des Plantes and returned to her seat in front of the mirror. She traced her stretch marks with her fingers and thought of all the magic creams and potions she'd rubbed into them to make them go away. She looked at the spread of her thighs and the dark hair between them and for the first time since she came to Yellowknife, she felt fully anchored in herself, a woman with a daughter and a history, a woman who took up space in the world. At the same time, she realized that she wasn't done yet with men and sex and pleasure.

"But I'm ample," she said. "From now on, I'm going to be ample."

She wiped her nose again, then got up and reached into the closet for a robe. Not the sexy one she wore for Bryan, but the comfortable fleece robe with the dribble of dried egg yolk down the front and the big pockets for Kleenex and cough drops. She put it on and pulled her thesaurus from the bookcase, sat down and looked up ample.

Abundant, bountiful, generous.

Celia smiled.

ANNELIES POOL, author of *Celia's Inner Anorexic*, has published numerous articles, columns and editorials in more than thirty Canadian periodicals and is a first place recipient of the Jack Sanderson Award for Editorial Writing. She is best known for the funny, personal columns which she has been writing for many years in various incarnations, the most recent of which was *Prelude Notes* in *above&beyond, Canada's Arctic Journal*. Annelies's first book *iceberg tea*,  a collection of her favourite columns, was published in 2010. In recent years Annelies has been exploring other genres. She is currently in the throes of writing a novel and when she's not busy with that, she serves as the executive director of NorthWords NWT.

Haunted Hill Mine

by Cathy Jewison

"Welcome to Haunted Hill Mine—last stop on our tour. Stay close as you exit the bus—don't want you to trip over a rock, or lose you down a hidden shaft."

"Oh my," said a scrawny white-haired woman in a bright pink tracksuit, the first to alight. "Certainly is … atmospheric." The horror that grew on her face as she surveyed the clearing in the boreal woods was more than Harold dared hope for—here, finally, was a client suitably spooked by the post-industrial gothic ambience of the site. Patches of wild grass alternated with clots of sand, piles of waste rock, scrap metal, scattered tires. A crude road cut across to the far side of the clearing, where tottered a couple of mouldering buildings and a half-rotted headframe. And past the headframe, the *pièce de resistance*: a large hill of beige rock into which had been blasted the main entrance of the mine. There it gaped, a giant maw guarded by iron bars, rusting like decaying teeth.

"Scary, eh?" Harold said.

The woman's friend, dressed in a matching outfit, pushed past. "It's a disgrace. Somebody ought to clean it up."

"Exactly what I was thinking," said the first woman, as she wandered away.

Next off the bus was a man wearing a flat tweed cap, who continually jotted notes on a pad of paper. "Oh, this place," he said. "Haunted Hill, my butt. This is the Snow Drop Mine. Guess 'Haunted Hill' looks better in the marketing materials."

Harold stood by the door of the minibus, giving a hand when needed, and enduring similar commentary as a half-dozen patrons of the Yellowknife Haunted History Tour disembarked. The final passenger appeared in the doorway—a woman with long, unnaturally black hair and jangly earrings. She paused, scrunching her eyes shut and taking a deep breath. As she exhaled, a hum sounded deep in her throat. She opened an eye and aimed it toward Harold. "I'm resonating. Attuning myself to the vibrations of the spirit world." Closing the eye, she resonated a couple more times before snapping back to the land of the living. "I sense nothing. There is no presence. This entire tour is a hoax. I'm reporting you to the Better Business Bureau."

"As it says on our website, and I've reminded you at our last three stops, the tour undertakes only to acquaint you with the *stories* of Yellowknife's haunted past. We guarantee no first-hand encounters with shades, phantoms, poltergeists, or other paranormal phenomena."

"Your stories are supposed to be *true*. If there was one shred of authenticity, I would pick up residual vibrations, at the very least. I'm highly intuitive." The woman swished off the bus and into the clearing, her India-print skirt swinging.

Harold watched her join the waiting group and launch into a diatribe. He groaned. The ghost tour business should have been a no-brainer—a tromp around the Yellowknife cemetery, a tour through the Old Town with a stop at the rapidly decaying House of Horrors up by Bush Pilots Monument … and the finale, a stopover at this decrepit little mine, a few kilometres outside of town. And yet, he was assailed on all sides: a recalcitrant clientele, payments for the minibus, exorbitant liability insurance, and "visitation fees" paid to his great-aunt Clara, the actual owner of the former-Snow-Drop-now-Haunted-Hill Mine.

The real threat, however, was the series of harassing phone calls he'd recently received about toxic waste at Haunted Hill. Small mines like this had once dotted the Yellowknife area, but they were almost all gone. Abandoned by their owners, the land was repossessed by the government, which, goaded by rabid environmentalists and a paranoid public, spent millions sealing the workings and razing the buildings.

That was the last thing Harold wanted. Fortunately, Aunt Clara had never let her leases lapse—she still owned the mining interests, as well as all the buildings and equipment on site, dilapidated as they were. Unfortunately, she'd recently been making noises about re-opening the mine. That was the second-last thing Harold wanted.

As he started toward the group, a piece of paper blew against his ankle. He leaned down to retrieve it. "Demand the immediate remediation of Haunted Hill Mine!" it screamed in large font. "Yellowknife's toxic time bomb!" The flyer sported a large photo of the mine's crumbling headframe, and carried the logo of a group of local tree-huggers known as "The Environmental Marauders."

"Frickin' fantastic," he muttered. He feared people could be easily swayed, sounding the death knell for his fledgling business. He scurried to retrieve several flyers that littered the ground, shoving them into his jacket pockets, before the poisonous idea could catch on.

On the plus side, however, it was a good day for a ghost tour—overcast and breezy. Harold herded the group up the dirt road and drew them into the darkness of the mine's entrance.

"Before I tell you the story of Haunted Hill, let's take a moment to soak in the ambience of the place."

Harold himself had always found the mine a little eerie, but the ghost tour crowd was a tough one, and he'd quickly learned that the experience needed enhancement. A discrete step on a wire tugged a nearby tree; the resident owl lifted from it and glided across the sky. The history buff, unfortunately, noticed the wire and shook his head. A burst of wind hit the clearing and a series of creaks and bangs sounded from the door on a rusting gym locker he'd installed behind the office building. Harold's reward should have been a shudder or two, a yelp of surprise, or even a collective frisson rippling through the crowd. Instead, people stared in various directions, while one of the track suit ladies—the mean one—used the toe of her runner to prod a muddy, industrial-sized battery. The black-haired psychic was swinging a large crystal suspended on a string and muttering gibberish.

Harold lit a kerosene lantern, and held it beside his head. He'd checked the pose in the bathroom mirror at home, and was satisfied that it cast an acceptably sinister shadow across his face. "Haunted Hill Mine was opened back in 1942 by Cecil Purdue. It's always been a family operation—Cecil and his wife Clara worked the site by themselves for a number of years."

"By themselves?" said the elderly malcontent, wiping the toe of her shoe with a tissue, which she tossed onto the ground. "That doesn't even make sense."

"Well, although the mine is small, it is reputed to have some of the richest ore bodies in the Yellowknife area."

"That much is true," said the historian.

Harold acknowledged this concession with a nod. "Cecil guarded his treasure carefully. He wanted no one outside the family to know the true riches of Haunted Hill Mine. As the ore was processed, he carefully hid away the gold—even Clara didn't know where he stashed it, but it is believed to be deep within the mine workings. Then the unthinkable happened—Cecil disappeared. It's believed he was working late one night, and stumbling through the dark, fell down a forgotten shaft."

"Or he took off to the Caribbean with one of the bar maids from the Gold Range Hotel," the man countered. "There are rumours."

There were also rumours that Clara had offed her philandering husband and dropped the body down one of the mine shafts herself. Harold kept silent on that count, partly because he was from Clara's side of the family, and partly because his future at Haunted Hill depended on Clara's good graces.

He continued. "Shortly thereafter, there were tales of strange sounds and sights—the slow, repeated clinks of a pick hitting rock deep in the mine workings when no one was there; phantom lights about this high," Harold held the kerosene lantern a couple of inches above his forehead, "the height of a headlamp on a miner's helmet. It's believed the spirit of Cecil Purdue still wanders underground, protecting his lost gold."

"Oh, for Pete's sake," said the old woman. "Ever heard of an echo? Or a reflection?"

Harold persevered. "Clara shut down the mine in 1949; it soon passed out of memory and has been lying deserted and forgotten. Until now."

"Actually, it's on the disused mine register," said a young man in a yellow Gore-Tex jacket. "Anyone can find it ... if they have a reason to look."

He waved an arm and another burst of wind ripped through the clearing. This time it belched up through the mine's main opening and spewed from the smaller shafts scattered through the site with stereophonic force. The crowd was unimpressed.

"That better not be a public address system," said the historian. "I'm going to look for wires."

"No—stop." Harold's sincerity surprised even himself. "I've never heard that before." He scanned the crowd, looking for someone who might be playing a hoax, maybe harbouring a tape recorder under their jacket. Most people were staring into space—except for the young man in yellow, who was staring at Harold, defiance on his face. There was also quite a lot of muck on his face, which was twisted sideways at a bizarre angle. Harold started. He didn't recognize the kid. A quick headcount showed there was an extra person in the group.

Ah, ha. The bloody environmentalist. He stepped toward the young man. The wind shifted and a wet flyer hit Harold in the face. He peeled it away to confront his nemesis—who'd vanished.

"Where'd he go?" Harold said.

"Who?" said the psychic.

"The guy in yellow. The one who was standing right beside you."

The woman rolled her eyes and followed the historian into the clearing. The rest of the group drifted away.

"Feel free to explore the site," Harold called after his patrons. "Maybe you can find Uncle Cecil's gold." He advised them to stick to the paths, as his insurance company had commanded him to do, thus reducing the possibility of someone twisting an ankle and suing him.

The snarky old lady flicked her head, just enough to let Harold know that she'd heard him, and took a short cut to the headframe, right through the grass. His premiums notwithstanding, he wouldn't mind seeing the earth swallow her whole.

Harold scanned the clearing and spotted the kid in yellow on the far side.

This was all he needed. He'd come up with the ghost tour gambit a couple of months earlier, when Aunt Clara had found him poking around the property. She claimed to be carrying out a "safety check," but Harold knew why she was really there. Her hunched figure, hobbling around the site, prodding the grates that covered the smaller mine shafts and checking to ensure that the bars guarding the main entrance were undisturbed, seemed less like a conscientious property owner and more like a troll protecting its treasure. Sixty years since the mine had closed, and she still hadn't found Cecil's legendary stash.

Her tone had been pleasant when she'd confronted her great-nephew, but he knew he'd better come up with something good. The nine-to-five thing hadn't been working for him, and he'd just been fired from his fifth job in a year. Pinning his financial future on the legend of the family gold was a long shot, perhaps, but rumours persisted. His impromptu ghost tour idea turned out to be an inspired one, because it ensured him access to the site. When he'd presented his proposal to Clara, she'd taken a moment to assess both Harold and the situation, then asked for a sizable cut. When Harold hesitated, she'd let it drop that she was planning to re-open the mine.

"You'd need a complete overhaul," Harold had said. "It'll cost a fortune."

"Already done the cost-benefit analysis," she'd said. "In this economy, gold's the only thing anyone can depend on." Her gaze had slid around the mangled landscape. "Unless you can turn a decent profit from your little tour, then I'd reconsider. But it would have to be worth my while."

Business had been good the first month, until it became obvious that Harold had nothing truly hair-raising to offer to a discerning ghost-seeking public. For the first time in his life, though, Harold was actually making an effort. His favourite part was the time he spent alone at the site, exploring and rigging up "improvements." In between tours, he'd search for the lost gold. He'd managed to loosen one of the iron bars at the main entrance, and had slipped down a couple of the tunnels to check things out.

And now this green freak was interfering with his attempts to earn an honest living. He high-tailed it across the mine site, the kerosene lamp still swinging at his side. From underneath the mud that still covered his face, the kid was positively glowering at him. Harold pulled up short and shook a fist full of flyers at him.

"What the hell?"

"Hell, indeed." A gesture of the kid's hand encompassed the mine site. "This is hell on earth, and it's your doing."

"Uncle Cecil's, actually."

"The sins of the fathers..." the kid intoned.

"*Un-cle*. Pay attention." The sneer on the kid's face, still set at that arrogant angle, made Harold's bile rise. He started toward him.

The kid threw up a hand. "Stop!"

His eyes were stretched open as far as possible and the muscles of his face were rigid. The chords of his neck popped out. He held the pose for a moment, then everything collapsed. He wiggled his jaw. "Crap—that hurt. So much for looking demonic."

"You're a regular hell-hound." Harold started forward again.

"Stop!"

"Or what?"

"Or you'll fall down that mine shaft."

Harold realized that the tall grass directly in front of him collapsed in on itself, ever so slightly. He set down the lantern, dropped to his knees and crawled forward. Parting the blades, he stared down into darkness. He gasped. "You took the grate. You little jerk. I'll fricking kill you."

The boy giggled. Harold pulled a flashlight from his jacket pocket. He shone it into the abyss, where it caught a spot of bright yellow about thirty feet down. He leaned in farther. Lying at the bottom of the shaft, face up, spread-eagle, was a body clothed in a bright yellow jacket. Its neck lay at a strange angle. He looked up at the kid.

"You got a twin?"

"Hardly."

Harold sat back on his heels. Maybe he *had* been spending too much time at the site. Maybe he was suffering from some strange type of industrial poisoning.

"Broke my neck on impact," the kid said.

That explained why his head flopped at such a strange angle.

"Die instantly?" Harold asked.

The kid nodded—awkwardly, given the state of his spinal column. "Didn't suffer. In case you care."

A death on the property. Harold had a sudden premonition. "Man, I don't have the nerves for this."

"Dealing with an actual ghost?"

"No—worrying about my liability insurance."

"Money—that's all your kind ever thinks about."

"Hey, hey. That's harsh."

"You know what's harsh? The crap coming out of this mine—acid draining from the workings, arsenic, cadmium, mercury. I have evidence."

Harold peered into the mine shaft. "You mean down there where no one can see it?"

The ghost took a sudden and intense interest in a small, smooth rock lying in the grass by his left foot.

"How long you been down there?" Harold asked.

The ghost poked the rock with his toe.

Harold snapped his fingers. "I'm talking to you."

The ghost sighed and looked up. "Three or four days."

"And no one's come looking for you?"

The game of footsie with the rock resumed.

"No one knows you're down there, do they?" A tempting thought occurred, but Harold beat it back. "Crap. I have to report it."

The ghost kicked aside the rock and met Harold's eyes, his face contorted as he attempted to look ominous once again. "And then you are going down. You and this abomination—this tour that celebrates the obscene exploitation of Mother Earth."

Harold hauled himself to his feet. "Very likely. I'm barely turning a profit. And my insurance will go through the roof."

The ghost eased his face out of menacing mode. As soon as his muscles would allow it, he smiled. "Excellent. I'll be back in their good books. I'll be a hero."

"Whose good books?" Harold picked up a stray flyer. "The Environmental Morons? Those losers? What was their latest 'action'? Pelting cars in downtown Yellowknife with rubber duckies?"

The ghost drew himself up as straight as his broken neck would allow. "I was bringing attention to the toxic mire known as the industrial tailings pond. Do you know how many waterfowl died on one in Alberta a couple of years ago?"

Harold laughed. "Was that you?"

"Can I help it if I have flair? All the rest of them want to do is make interventions at regulatory hearings. As if. Take it to the streets, I say."

"That you did. There were squished duckies all over downtown for weeks. You really should learn not to litter." Harold flourished the flyer to reinforce the point.

The ghost snatched it from Harold and smoothed it against his leg. "The Maurauders said I was a drama queen. Hurting their corporate image. They'll be mad I used their logo—they told me not to. But shutting down the tour and forcing a clean-up of the mine would be a real coup. My name will live on."

"Oh, your name will live on all right," Harold said. "As the person responsible for the re-opening of the Snow Drop Mine."

"Say what?"

"My aunt wants money, and if she doesn't get enough from me, she'll start digging again. Congratulations—I'll make sure your granola-munching buddies know all about it."

"She can't! The pollution! Oh, crap! Why does everything always go wrong?" The ghost paced, working himself into a full-fledged tantrum. He started to moan. He found a length of chain, long abandoned in the grass, and whipped it back and forth. The combined racket of his howls and the rattle of the chain grew until it filled the clearing.

And then it happened. One of the old ladies jumped. Several of the tour group shuddered. Even the pseudo-psychic stopped in her tracks.

"Hey," Harold said. "You *do* have flair."

The kid preened.

Harold watched his clients wandering over the broken ground, searching for the source of the disturbance. "I should cut my losses anyway. The hidden gold's a non-starter. Clara wouldn't let people onto the property if there was the least hope it existed. She's even stopped her safety patrols."

"Oh, she wasn't out here looking for the gold. She's keeping tabs on Cecil. Or what's left of him."

Harold's head swivelled toward the ghost. "No way!"

"Way. He's in a stope on the far side. All this time in all that acid. Even the bones are pretty much gone. That's probably why she thought it was safe to let people down there again."

"Still—she must have got the gold."

The ghost grinned and gave a little shrug. "She might not have got it all. In any case, there's probably enough of Cecil's DNA lying around to convince Clara to postpone her plans. You can keep running your business. I'm sure you have bills to pay."

The raven-haired psychic marched over. Harold noticed she was trembling. "I'm not sure how you did that, but it's creeping me out."

"Well, it is a ghost tour."

"So you say. I'm outta here." She turned and marched toward the bus.

Harold and the ghost exchanged a look.

"Come on, it'll be fun," the ghost said.

"That's true. And I was thinking about doing something spooky with the headframe." Harold peered down the mine shaft one last time. "You're sure?"

"Absolutely. And no need to mention my … uh … situation to anyone."

Harold dug around in the grass until he found the grate. He slipped it over the mine shaft and headed for the bus.

CATHY JEWISON, author of *Haunted Hill Mine*, has had a career focused on the written word—she's worked as a newspaper reporter, copy editor and government communicator. After moving to Yellowknife in 1986, Cathy dabbled in poetry, drama, and creative non-fiction, but settled on the short story as her preferred literary form. Since then, her quirky characters have appeared on the pages of magazines and anthologies. Cathy's first book, a collection of stories, set in Yellowknife, *The Ugly Truck and Dog Contest and Other Tales of Northern Life*, was published by Borealis Press in 2009.

My Epiphany
by Rebecca Aylward

I was a little worried, a little annoyed, and in quite the foul mood. My uncle wanted to leave by noon. I was worried because I was sure I was at least fifteen minutes late, and I did not want to make him angry or annoyed with me before we even started out. I had some difficulty finding the key for my snowmobile, and then I had some trouble getting it started. Besides all of that, I was in a foul mood because I really did not want to be tackling such a chore in the first place. It was Saturday. It was freezing out. It was the first day of the holiday break from my teaching job.

I pulled into his driveway exactly twenty minutes past twelve. To my relief, he was still packing supplies into one of the sleds. I allowed my machine to idle. I fumbled with my helmet and pulled on my toque. I trudged over to where my uncle was working to offer him some help.

Uncle Louie motioned towards a brightly painted wooden box on his front steps. He assumed that I would understand that he meant for me to bring it over to one of the sleds we would be hauling. My uncle is a man of few words, but I have come to learn to do as I am sometimes not told.

Before I picked up the box, I peeked inside. I was surprised by my uncle's foresight and thoughtfulness. Food, utensils, toilet paper and other things I never would have even thought to bring, filled what I now knew to be his grub box.

Uncle moved his snowmobile so that I could back mine up to the other sled. He hooked up the near-empty sled to my machine, got onto his and started to pull out of the driveway. Again, I struggled with my helmet, and then I gave the snowmobile some gas so I could catch up. I remembered to turn wide at the last minute so that I was centered on the trail.

On the trail ride, I was alone inside my helmet with my thoughts.

About a month ago, Uncle Louie had dropped off a nice load of firewood. I thanked him, helped him stack it and half-heartedly offered to help the next time he was going out for some. Now here I was.

Several minutes after we turned into the bush, Uncle pulled over and began to unload some supplies. He exchanged helmet for fur hat, grabbed his chainsaw and made his way over to some trees. I watched as he chose his targets one by one. I noticed that the trees he cut looked either dead, nearly-dead or were leaning over pitifully.

At this point, I was not sure how I was going to help and there was no asking over the steady and noisy roar of the chainsaw. I stood shivering and waiting. I thought about my duvet, the book I was reading and about what I was going to do after all this.

After four or five trees were cut down, Uncle turned off the chainsaw and told me to bring the big axe over. I was nearly winded from trudging my way over to where he was standing. The problem wasn't the distance, but the nature of the snow. The snow was like tiny styrofoam balls—the kind that will not pack down no matter how often one walks over it. The snow would shift temporarily out of your way as you plowed through it, but it would return to its original state as soon as you had passed.

I handed the axe over to my mother's only brother and he taught me how to knock the branches off the tree with the blunt side of the axe. Uncle then told me to do the same to the rest of the cut down trees.

I was happy to have a purpose. I dutifully worked my way down the fallen tree and got nearly halfway down the second when I heard the chainsaw roar to life again. Uncle was now slicing the log into foot-long chunks behind me. Once he caught up to me on the third tree, the chainsaw got another rest and he walked back to the sled.

"Finish the branches and then put those cut ones by the sleds," ordered my uncle. He took a small axe and some other things I couldn't see and disappeared into the bush a little further along the clearing.

About a half an hour later, my uncle emerged from the bush and came back to get me. By this time, I had managed to haul most of the wood over to where the sleds sat. Making my way through the snow was exhausting. The work was physical and repetitive. I wondered what excuse I might be able to come up with to go home.

"Come and take a break," invited my uncle.

I happily followed him back to a small clearing, sheltered from the wind. He had started a fire and set up some stumps for us to sit on. In between the stumps sat the grub box, and its hinged lid opened fully to serve as a table for our break.

I was tired and sweating, so I removed my jacket and gloves. Although it was hovering around minus thirty-four, I was comfortable and ready to relax.

Uncle added some snow to the pot on the fire, and told me to do the same once it melted down and to call him back once it was boiling.

I poked around in the grub box and found what I needed to prepare a couple of Klik and bannock sandwiches. Once that was done, I stood and watched the pot on the fire. While I waited, I listened to the fire, the wind and the distant and distinct chopping sound of the axe. My mind was unoccupied with work, so I began to think about things.

I wondered if anyone had ever stood exactly where I was standing now, doing exactly what I was doing. I would say yes, but without the luxury of a chainsaw, matches and a snowmobile. I stared at the fire and wondered how my ancestors started fires without lighters or matches. I wondered what they wore when it got this cold. I wondered how they could have survived without the amenities I thought necessary to survive in the north: a shelter, seasonal clothing, running water, and a grocery store. Suddenly I was full of questions and wonderment. I felt a deep and overwhelming respect and admiration for those who came before me. I might not be here if my ancestors had not found a way to survive and thrive.

Soon the water reached a boil and I called out to my uncle. He returned to our makeshift camp with eyebrows, moustache and eyelashes full of frost. Uncle removed the boiling water from the fire and placed four teabags into the pot. I rummaged through the grub box once more and found two mugs, some sugar and a spoon.

I asked my uncle about how they started fires long ago, and he replied with a story that did not really answer my question. While he recalled his boyhood, we fixed ourselves a cup of tea and began to eat our sandwiches. I listened thoughtfully as Uncle recalled his experiences with collecting firewood as a boy. I could tell that we grew up in very different circumstances.

We had a woodstove in the house where I grew up. The firewood we used to heat our home was purchased and delivered to our driveway. Had I not brought in enough wood as a teenager, the furnace would have to kick in and I might get a scolding. If he had done the same, someone would have to go out and get more. There was no other source of heat.

I listened to my uncle's recollections and became a little ashamed of myself. I never knew how hard it was for our family back then. Everyone had to contribute because it was necessary. I thought about my contribution as a child and now as an adult. What had I done to help meet our family's basic needs? I thought about my grumbling and whining and the sheer laziness of my youth, and I was embarrassed.

I started to stare at my feet. I was about to tell my uncle how I was feeling, but I noticed him getting up from the stump. The time for talking was now over. He headed back to our cache of firewood and left me at the fire. There was no way I was going to continue sitting, though I was still tired and felt like having more tea.

I got up from my stump, and began to pack the grub box. I washed our cups and utensils with some soap and water Uncle had already boiled. I snuffed out the fire with some snow, and carried each stump over to my uncle so he could chop them. I returned the grub box to the sled and then began to help my uncle again.

We packed one sled full of split firewood, and the other with our supplies. We worked quickly and quietly. Uncle showed me how to tie the tarps so that the wood would not fall out on our trip home. We started our snowmobiles and gave them a chance to warm up somewhat. Uncle said that we could share the firewood we collected that day, and that we would drop off his share and the supplies on the way to my house. We put on our helmets and drove back the way we came several hours earlier.

On the way back to Uncle's house, I found myself alone inside my helmet with my thoughts.

We pull into Uncle's driveway at four-thirty. I helped him unload everything and told him that he should keep the whole load of firewood for himself. I said, "Maybe we can go get some firewood for me next weekend."

REBECCA AYLWARD, author of *My Epiphany*, is an educator, living and working in the community of Hay River where she has resided since birth. She lives with her partner Ken and their two-year-old daughter. Rebecca enjoys writing about the north because of the special places and people she encounters there. She is curious about her history and culture and she likes writing with those interests in mind. Rebecca has another story published in *Many Voices, Many Journeys: An Anthology of Stories by Aboriginal Teachers*.

Jailbird

by Patti-Kay Hamilton

Justice of the Peace Bobby Britain was red-faced and losing his patience. I was challenging a fifty-dollar fine the bylaw officer had issued when he spotted my dog running at large in Yellowknife's Old Town. I argued that the officer had no evidence because he hadn't caught my pet. He didn't even have a photo of him. It could have been someone else's dog.

The courtroom above the Post Office stank of damp mukluks and was crowded with more serious offenders including an old friend charged with pissing alongside a Mountie's car in front of the Gold Range Bar. The JP was keen to move on to these more important matters. He called my complaint frivolous and refused to buy my argument. He insisted I pay the fine. I refused. I was saving for a trip to Vancouver and there was no way I was going to part with fifty bucks.

"I'll take the jail time." I said.

His jowls jiggling, he snarled, "You can't go to jail for your dog running at large."

I responded haughtily as if I knew what I was talking about, "Then the Justice system isn't fair to the poor." He let out a kind of growl and dismissed me with "Two days in Women's Corrections. Enjoy."

Female inmates were housed in a musty-smelling old trailer. It was beside the male-only jail. At first I was chuckling to myself thinking this would be a lark but as steel doors clanged shut behind me I started to have second thoughts. A butchy, grey-haired lady who looked like a former nun I'd known took my fingerprints and mug shot and led me to my cell. It was small but more comfortable and warmer than some places I'd lived. In the kitchen I met the only other inmates. Two tough-looking girls from the Mackenzie Delta. Bertha was tiny and toothless. She was tapping into the prison system's medical benefits and had arranged to have all her teeth removed. She'd been waiting two months for her dentures. Addy was a big Gwich'in gal with a scar that slashed across her nose and cheeks. They were doing time for stealing the cash register from the Hudson Bay store in their hometown. They might have gotten away with it but they were spotted when they threw the machine into the Mackenzie River and it floated. Their take was $75.

The ladies had cooking privileges so they could bake bannock and traditional food if someone dropped off caribou meat. They seemed unusually enthusiastic about cleaning their own bathroom. They pointed to the out of order sign on one of the two stalls and told me not to go in there. We spent a lot of time in the TV room watching soaps and darning socks. Darning wasn't a skill I'd learned in the Toronto suburb where I grew up but since we got paid for it I happily picked up the wooden ball and needle and reached into the pile of men's socks. I found the soaps boring but the girls were not. Something happens among women doing busy, quiet work like stitching or picking cranberries, even in prison. It begins with casual chatter and gossip and grows into a revealing exchange about things troubling to the soul.

There was a reason these girls were scarred inside and out. My stomach turned as they described their experiences as little children at the Grollier Hall Residential School in Inuvik. In a moment of quiet I asked Addy about her scar. As she spoke it was obvious that the incident had cycled like a video in her memory since it happened.

She'd been six years old, playing tag in a large common room with her best friend. They'd ignored the supervising nun's command to be quiet and ran around the wood stove in the centre of the room, colliding and giggling as they hugged each other. The sister grabbed each of them by the hair and held their faces against the red hot stove.

Bertha lifted up her long hair to show me a damaged ear lobe. One of the sisters had disciplined her by grabbing her ear and dragging her up the stairs to her room. The skin connecting the ear was torn from the side of her head. She'd fallen asleep crying with the blood from the wound soaking her pillow. She was only eight.

I was humbled by their stories of survival. I also felt guilty. I recalled as a child lining up to give money to a missionary who'd appealed to us at a school assembly to help the poor pagan Indian and Eskimo children in the north. I wondered if Bertha and Addy were in any of the photos she'd shown.

We had to walk to the cafeteria in the men's jail for meals. The male inmates were on their way out as we entered. Freddie, a grizzled old diamond driller who was serving a long sentence for a real crime punched me in the shoulder on the way by and muttered, "Hey kid. What'd they bust you for? Dope?" I wanted to nod. I was tempted to invent a more interesting offense because if I admitted to my dog running at large he might resent my impersonating a jailbird. I chose to hang my head in silence.

The girls had a surprise for me on my last night in jail. It was shift change and the guards were behind closed doors in the office. Addy handed me a chipped, green melmac mug and told me to go into the stall with the broken toilet and lift the lid off the tank. My hands were shaking as I took the cup. Was this where I got my lumps for being a naive white girl mocking the jailhouse experience? They followed close behind and we crowded into the tiny stall. When I lifted the lid it looked and smelled like bubbling swamp water with brown scum on top. I looked back at Bertha. "Homebrew," she whispered.

My resourceful new friends had disabled the toilet by cracking the tank, draining the water, plugging the crack and lining it with green garbage bags. Using their cooking privileges, they'd gathered yeast, raisins, and sugar and mixed them with warm water to make Jailhouse Brew. Since the women were responsible for the bathroom clean-up, the guards seldom entered their john and never questioned the out of order sign on the door. The three of us dipped our cups and slurped back the raw tasting fluid. It was a potent blend and we soon felt the buzz. In the TV room we hung out the window whistling and taunting the male inmates who were working outside. Just as we were inviting the boys for a kiss and more I was grabbed by my braid and dragged into the cell by the matron.

Annie was a big, tough Métis woman with a don't-mess-with-me look on her face. She slammed the door. "Glad you're enjoying your stay. You'll be with us for the rest of the weekend."

The hangover the next morning was more painful than the penalty for being drunk in jail. But the next few days were like penance. I was restless, feeling caged and wanting to get outside. It was spring. The sun was shining, snow was melting. I could hear the crystalline tinkling of candled ice from the nearby creek. It was Caribou Carnival weekend. I wanted to be at the finish line of the Dog Derby flirting with the nice-looking musher from Fort Resolution. I wanted to be at the Longest Bar drinking Caribou Blood, a cocktail of red wine and vodka while jigging to the flying fiddles of the Native Cousins. Instead I was stuck inside darning and watching soaps. Bertha told me that's how she felt in residential school: like you were a trapped animal looking out the window at everyone else leading a normal life and no one showing up to spring the trap.

When I was released I received a cheque for fifty-five dollars for my darning. I was one hundred and five dollars richer than if I'd paid the fine and I had two new friends. To celebrate I went to the downtown store owned by Justice of the Peace Britain. I bought a chocolate Easter bunny. With a nursing friend's syringe I injected hash oil into the rabbit, repackaged it and mailed it to my jailbird buddies. I couldn't spring their trap but I could show up and let them know I would stay connected.

PATTI-KAY HAMILTON, author of *Jailbird* is perhaps best known as a host, reporter and producer with CBC North. For thirty years she shared the stories and adventures of northern people. In 1985 she was a member of the team that won the Gabriel Award for excellence in radio journalism. Peter Gzowski praised Hamilton as a poet and a storyteller during an interview with Pamela Wallin on CTV.

Before joining CBC Hamilton ran a dogteam on a trapline, worked as a river guide and baked butter tarts in her log home and delivered them to the Wildcat Café by skiff. She studied drama at the National Theatre School and creative writing at both the University of Guelph and Calgary. Since retiring Hamilton has been working on a collection of short stories based on life around Yellowknife's Old Town in the 70s as well as several theatre projects. She lives in Fort Smith where she skis and paddles as much as possible with her husband and black lab.

Homecoming

by Cara Loverock

Looking out his window into the horizon Eli's mind turned to his son Mason. It would be three years tomorrow that the search for his only child was given up. Mason had been a proud hunter, living off the land. He hunted caribou, muskox, and polar bear.

It was still clear in Eli's mind the way his son looked as he prepared for another season's hunt. Mason had hunted many times before, every winter since he was fourteen. Mason was wearing his blue parka trimmed with wolf fur and his mittens, worn and tattered only halfway into the winter season. He also had his survival gear: a stove, blankets and the like.

"I'll be back in a few days, maybe a week depending on the weather," Mason had said just before he drove off on his snowmobile.

Eli sat down in the kitchen, and the sadness began to seep in and take hold of him. The wind swept up the snow so that it swirled as it hit against the house, sounding like the sand inside a rattle. It seemed that no matter how much time passed, the torture of missing Mason would never get easier. Every day was like swimming in a pool of grief, and Eli splashed wildly just to keep from drowning in it.

The elderly man couldn't stop hoping that one day Mason would show up, a little worse for wear. He could imagine he had somehow survived in the bush all this time. Eli remembered how proud he was when his only son came back from his first hunt. He had taken down a muskox with an Enfield rifle.

Life in the arctic was different. There were no shopping malls; the youth weren't obsessed with video games, the Internet and cell phones. Not that they were cut off from the modern world—it was just a different kind of modern.

Mason had disappeared in March. It was a month when the sun still wasn't quite coming up. The town was plunged into darkness for what sometimes felt like forever. Swallowed whole by winter. The community's spirit was always raised when a hunter came back with food to share, like muskox or caribou. A few years before Mason had shown up after six days gone with a muskox that some said was the size of a bus. Eli had beamed with pride.

A few days after he had failed to return, a Twin Otter carrying spotters was dispatched. Soon after a Hercules aircraft came all the way from Ontario. But then the search had to be put on hold as a blizzard rolled through the region.

The words of the RCMP officer still rang in his ears. The search for Eli's boy was no longer a rescue mission, but a recovery mission. Eli was so tired. He had barely slept for weeks. How could this be? His son was strong, a skilled hunter. He knew the land.

Hope faded. The community held a memorial on the lake. Mason's wife Sarah stood on the ice with her and Mason's small daughter.

Eli had slipped on the ice during the ceremony. He had fallen hard and hit his head, causing a mild concussion. He reached back and felt the spot on his skull where the bump had formed when he fell. It was long gone now. He sat down and poured himself some scotch.

He had been ten years sober before Mason's disappearance. Eli had stopped drinking after he was caught driving drunk through town. He learned what had happened when the facts were read aloud in the tiny community centre that acted as a makeshift courthouse. Eli had sat red-faced, embarrassed to hear that he had been weaving down the main road. One of the community's two police officers had come out to get him. Eli had staggered out of his truck and over to the officer, nearly falling down. "I don't sell drugs!" Eli shouted at him. He had pissed himself and the officer found an empty twenty-sixer of beer in the back of the truck. It was mostly empty. Eli was too drunk to remember what happened. He only recalled waking up on the cold floor of the single jail cell in the RCMP detachment. His head was pounding, his pants were wet through, and there was a sickening stench of urine.

It had been Eli's third time caught drunk behind the wheel. The large fine and humiliation, not to mention having his licence taken away for more than a year, wasn't the example he wanted to set for his son, a teenager at the time.

A knock at the door snapped Eli out of his daydream. Sarah was at the door. She let herself in as usual.

"Eli! Looks like a blizzard might be comin'," she called out. Mason's daughter took a seat on the floor. Eli studied her, searching for his son in the little girl's face. There was another knock at the door.

"Who is that?" Eli asked Sarah.

"I don't know, go find out," she replied. Eli opened the front door to find his friend George standing there.

"Hey Eli. Myrna made this for the little one," he said. George held out a sealskin doll that looked like an owl.

"Brought some bannock too," he said.

"C'mon in George," said Eli. Eli looked at George who had a strange expression on his face. It gave Eli an uneasy feeling.

George had some understanding of losing someone to the land. A late season blizzard had killed his niece. She had ventured out onto the tundra where she was found frozen to death.

"What's going on? You want to go play bridge later at the community centre?" Eli asked. George was visibly uncomfortable.

"They uncovered a body, near Sachs Harbour. They think it's a good chance it's Mason," George said, feeling instantly alienated once the words were out of his mouth. Eli looked at Sarah. The tears began to well up in her eyes.

"It matched the description?" Eli asked.

"Yeah," George said.

Eli felt a sense of peace for the first time in years. Mason was coming home.

CARA LOVEROCK, author of *Homecoming*, attended the University of Toronto where she studied English literature and then went to Sheridan College for journalism. She spent ten years working as a print journalist, writing for various magazines and newspapers. In recent years Cara has been trying her hand at fiction writing, with a couple of short story credits to her name so far. A native of Ottawa, she lives in Yellowknife with her husband Mike and their two dogs.

Dirty Rascal

by Christine Raves

Danny and I haven't said a thing to each other since leaving my house. We're supposed to be doing our homework. It's the only reason his mom let him out tonight.

"Are we really going to use any of this when we're older?" He wanted to go for a walk instead.

"But it's winter outside," I reminded him. He rolled his eyes and sighed before throwing me a toque from the basket in the closet.

When I saw Travis waiting at the end of my driveway, I understood why Danny came over in the first place. Travis is his friend these days, ever since he moved to town a month ago. They hang out at break, skip school to sit in the coffee shop and talk about music and Bernice Foundering's big chest. They were in the coffee shop instead of gym class when Danny's mom caught him, and he's been grounded ever since.

Under a streetlight close to the big lake, Danny digs into his jacket pocket and pulls out a cigarette. It's broken in half and covered in lint.

"Easy fix," says Travis, taking it. He pinches tobacco from the middle and twists one end until the sides fit together again.

"Where'd you get that?" I ask.

Danny shrugs. "I stole it."

"You stole it?"

"My dad doesn't notice if I only take one at a time."

"Not a big bad cigarette!" interrupts Travis. "You might get in trouble!" Danny laughs.

A dark brown van passes us, music blaring through closed windows and frozen steel. A group of girls are laughing, fists pumping, before they leave us with red tail lights and a flashing right-hand signal as the van heads up the main avenue.

Travis pulls out a red Bic lighter. The flame blows out no matter how he tries to shelter it from the wind. Click, click, click. He swears and shoves everything into his pockets.

"It never got this cold where I used to live. Yellowknife sucks. Let's go to the arcade, already." Danny agrees even though he knows the arcade is for high schoolers and drug dealers.

Travis sees me hesitate. "Aww, you're not allowed?"

"Danny's not allowed to go either."

Danny glares. "I'm allowed to do what I want."

I know he'll leave me behind if I don't suggest another place we could go. "Let's sneak over to the castle instead. I bet it's really creepy at night."

"The what?" Travis doesn't know what I'm talking about, but Danny does. "I haven't been there in forever."

Between the moon and the city lights, I can make out every angle of the castle. It sparkles the closer we get, a constellation in its own right. It seems as solid as concrete but is as temporary as the snow it's made of. In the spring the castle will melt. But tonight, still under construction, there are arches over doorways, windows made of ice, towers shaped like cones, and gargoyles keeping watch from the high walls.

"What is this?" asks Travis.

"It's the Snowking Castle."

"In the middle of nowhere? What's the point?"

"He builds it for people. You know, to see and stuff."

"That's messed up. There's not even a fence around it."

Danny shakes his head. He's not exactly smiling, but there's a trace of something there. "I forgot all about this place."

"How long since you were last here?" I ask.

"Whenever your mom last took us, I think."

"Well," says Travis. "If this crazy guy builds this thing for everyone, we should probably check it out." He nudges me forward. "You first."

There are no lights on at the houseboats nearest the castle, so I guide us through an unlocked door, under the main archway, into a dark and narrow hallway where we're protected from the wind. Without looking behind me, I know Danny has to hunch so that his head doesn't hit the ceiling. I stop when we're all through the door, as if one more step turns us from visitors to intruders. "Maybe this is far enough. Someone might see us."
Travis shoves me forward. "Don't be such a baby." I keep walking.

There's a large room without a roof at the end of the hallway. We stand in a circle as Travis strikes the lighter. His face glows when he brings the flame to the cigarette between his lips. He keeps the lighter on, turns it sideways so he doesn't burn his thumb and gives the cigarette to Danny who takes a drag. Tilting his head back, Danny exhales smoke through his nostrils. I watch them share back and forth. I stick out my hand. Danny stares at me like I have two heads, but Travis gives it to me with a smirk on his face. The cigarette feels awkward no matter how I try to hold it. I settle on pinching it between my thumb and index finger. *Don't cough*. But I'm gasping for air the second I inhale.
"Pussy," whispers Travis. Danny sighs and takes the cigarette from me before slapping me on the back.
"Let's split up and see if we find anything worth keeping," says Travis. "Me and Dan will go back through the front. You go over there." He's pointing to another hallway at the far end of the room. I head towards it, but return once they're gone. When my eyes re-adjust to the darkness, I recognize a flight of stairs in the corner. They twist all the way to the top of the castle and lead to a slide.
I remember when Danny and I came to the castle that first time. We were seven years old. We half-climbed, half-pulled each other all

the way up the stairs to slide down together, holding on tight through our snowsuits. We did this over and over until our legs were too tired to lift us anymore.

Crawling up one stair at a time, I listen for him now. He better not have left me here, the jerk. The cold filters through my pants the moment I sit, so I move quickly and give myself a hard push. I'm whipping down and around as the slide plunges and turns. It's a lot faster than I expect. I howl as I throw my arms up to fly and fall all at the same time. The entire thing lasts for maybe three seconds before I'm left sprawled on the ground.

"What the hell!" Danny's face appears over mine. "Why were you screaming? I thought you were being chased by the cops or something."

I'm giggling like I'm a little girl. I can't help it. "You should go on that slide." Danny doesn't answer.

"What's wrong?" I ask.

He gestures with his arm. "This place is smaller than I remember. I thought it would be bigger with a million different doorways and hallways. When we were kids, it felt like the castle walls never ended. I thought the Snowking was some sort of wizard and this place was built with magic." Danny shakes his head quickly. "That seems so stupid now."

"Try the slide," I tell him again. Really though, I'm begging. *Go on the slide, Danny. Just once.* He shuffles from side to side like he's considering it until Travis walks in and points at me lying on the ground. "I told you he was probably fine." Then he holds up a shovel. "Finders, keepers."

I'm confused until he aims it at the castle wall. "Hey!" I yell.

Travis steps closer, lowers the shovel, and leans over me. I can smell the cigarette smoke on his breath. "You need to shut your mouth."

When the metal hits the wall, all three of us expect the entire thing to crash down, but there's barely a dent. The strength of the castle makes Travis more determined. He aims again and hits the wall over and over.

"Let's go already," says Danny. "I'm cold."

Travis follows us, dragging the shovel behind him. When we're outside, he examines the arch above the main entrance. The carved wedges are stacked against each other to form a semi-circle so perfect that it must take more than magic to craft.

"Hey Danny," says Travis. "Watch this." He stretches high to attack the middle block of the archway. Snow dust covers his face. I tug on Danny's arm because Travis won't ever listen to me. "He's going to ruin it." Danny sighs and steps away from me. He takes the shovel from Travis in one easy grab. I'm relieved and ready to go home. But Danny says, "My turn." And with his back to me, he takes the final swing.

As if connected by an invisible string, the falling block pulls the rest of the arch with it. It's about to land on their heads, but they back up at the last second. Travis cheers. Danny finally looks at me. "Go home, Sam."

They aren't done. They won't be until the castle is ruined.

"Yeah, Sam," adds Travis. "No one wants you here, anyway."

Danny finds every archway. Travis climbs the scaffolding and kicks the gargoyles one by one. They tip over ice sculptures, stomp on fallen blocks, piss on white walls. This is all a stupid story they'll tell tomorrow, and if they get into trouble, it will be together, while I just stand here and watch it all tumble down.

CHRISTINE RAVES, author of *Dirty Rascal,* has had her work published in *Room* and Yellowknife's 'zine *Do It Up.* Recently, she completed a twenty-two-week Wired Writing Studio program through the Banff Centre under the mentorship of author Alissa York. Christine has lived in Yellowknife for twenty-five years and doesn't understand why anyone would ever want to leave, especially since the Snowking really does build a giant castle every winter.

The Long Gun
by Shawn McCann

I was a very good girl until I was sixteen (and that's pretty old to stay a good girl in this place). I never went to a house party, I never shared a bottle up on Tin Can Hill where everyone partied when it was warm enough. I heard about the parties and what happened at them, but I never went because I wasn't invited, or more likely because I never understood that there were types of parties that you didn't need an invite to attend.

I was lonely, but the thing about a small town is if you never leave, there aren't a lot of opportunities for reinvention. It's hard to make friends with a person you've vaguely known your entire life. There's a lot of transience around here, but potential new friends were usually either snapped up immediately by more popular kids, or clearly undesirable themselves.

Jessee finally broke my loop of loneliness, just before my sixteenth birthday. She was new, from the Okanagan valley, and fell on the desirable side of most kids' judgement scales but she had another quality that few kids who grow up moving between small communities have. She really, truly didn't give a fuck what anyone thought. She had strong opinions about what she liked, and she could make friends with almost anyone because something they did was interesting to her. When she'd been in town for a few days, she commented on a *Ned's Atomic Dustbin* patch I had on my backpack. We started talking about music, and ended up hanging out after school.

Within a week, I found myself following her and Missy Pye down the Frame Lake trail towards a party at Flat Richard's. We were sharing a horrible mixture of booze we'd snuck by mixing together single shots off the tops of all the liquor bottles at Missy's parents. It was an awful opaque brown colour, and included rum, rye, vodka, some sort of brandy, crème de cacao and some sort of strawberry liquor from a recent trip to Cancun. It was really too horrible to drink, but we were taking turns sipping it back and had ourselves convinced we were already wrecked.

It was weird for me to be hanging out with Missy Pye. We had been friends once, when we were small enough to still play Barbies. Then one fall she'd shown up at the first day of school in a crop top and Fancy Ass jeans, made out with both the hot guys named Troy before the end of the first week, and we'd never really talked since then.

"Sooo, Bets, who you going for tonight?" I was dumbstruck by the question. Jessee was asking me as if I went for someone every week, like Missy. As if it wasn't completely outside the realm of possibility that some boy, likely who I'd known since he had duct tape on the knees of his snowpants, would be interested in making out with me. Did she not realize I was completely undesirable? That I was commonly referred to as 'Narc' or 'big brain glasses face' in particularly tender moments?

It's really important to be clear here that I was interested in the boys. I wanted to go for them, almost every single one of them, even the ones who mocked my clothes and made fun of what a prude I was. If only they knew the things I was ready to do with them in back hallways. I had a crush for every class of the day, and a particular place in my heart—and when I was particularly honest with myself—in my pants, for Flat Richard.

Ah, Flat Richard. Whose very house we were nearing by the minute. So called because at his first house party in seventh grade, he had passed out flat in the middle of the floor before anyone had arrived. I hadn't been there, of course, but other kids described posing over him like a large bearskin rug, and he did have the huge, raw-boned, loose limbs of a bear. He was beautiful. His dad was somebody important in government, and my mom had once referred to his mom as a "Dene princess." They had a lot of money and a big huge house, and they were nearly never home. Flat Richard was friends with everybody, and somehow, even when he made fun of my corduroy pants and called me 'whitey' I felt special.

"Does Bets actually talk?" said Missy, breaking the silence following Jess's question.

"Fuck you," I added helpfully.

"Wow, bitchy much? I was just going to say I heard Flat Richard say he was glad you were finally breaking out of your ice palace and coming out with Missy and me tonight. You should really...." Here Jess took a big gulp of swamp water and started sputtering. I never heard the rest of what she had to say because we were now at his door.

You know when you are a kid, and it is Christmas morning, and it's early and dark and cold, and you are so nervously excited that your body is shaking and everything around you is super defined? That was the way I felt walking through that door.

There were boots all over the front hall, and so many people—more than I had guessed would be there—more than I realized there were of the right age in the city ... and some of them really weren't the right age, in my mind. We pushed our way in through the huge recessed living room and the first person I recognized was Mike, a maintenance man from my dad's business. Way too old to be here (in his twenties at least!) and openly checking out Missy's cleavage. Gross.

"Hey Bets. Hey Missy, where you been?" Mike held out a couple of beers to us. I panicked a bit, but Missy and Jess just grabbed them and kept moving into the kitchen. All around me, faces were familiar, but I didn't know who or where to stop at, so I just kept going. I wound my way through the kitchen, into a back rec room area where the Troys and a bunch of other guys from class were playing pool and ignoring their girlfriends, and up the stairs into a big open hallway that didn't seem to have any purpose except for displaying large mounted animal heads. The area was fairly clear, so I thought it would be safe to stop.

Too late I realized I had found myself exactly where I was most afraid to be, directly in front of Flat Richard, who was attempting to hold up Tara Martin by the elbows.

"Ellllizzabettth!" Tara shrieked, as if I was her long-lost best friend. She was clearly very, very drunk, and fell over onto me as Flat Richard dropped her arms.

"Um, hi?" I managed to squeeze out, sounding like a valley girl on helium. Nice. Here was Flat Richard whom I loved, clearly about to get somewhere with one of the hottest girls in school, and I couldn't even sound like a normal person. This was all exactly wrong, and I needed to get out of the way fast. I tried to nudge Tara back over to Richard, and back myself away, but he reached out for my arm instead.

"Bits. Bits. Tara is having a bit of a rough time tonight. I need your help." He looked me straight in the eye. "Are you sober?"

"Uh. Yeah?" I squeaked again.

"I'm so glad you're here. You need to keep Tara out of trouble. Danny saw her making out with one of the Troys and got all weird and possessive, and I gotta get him out of here and find a way to get her home safe."

Here Tara interrupted in a slurred moan—"He's gonna killll me."

"Bits—are you good with her? Take her somewhere quiet and away from Danny and Troy. Now."

What the fuck was this? Is this what it was like to be at a party? Was this what I had been missing all these years? I grabbed Tara by the arm and started pulling her back down the stairs. I figured I could bring her into the heated garage I had noticed off to one side.

"No, Elllizabethh. I neeeed a drenk. A drenk. I wannahavesumfun." Jesus. There was a cooler at the edge of the garage. I sat her down on it.

"Okay, give me a second, I'll get you a drink." I was pretty sure when someone was that drunk you were supposed to give them water. I probably learned that in SADD. I dumped a cup of mystery liquid sitting on the edge of the stairs, and ran out of the garage into the nearest bathroom to fill it with water.

I felt like I was moving really quickly, but apparently not fast enough. I came around the corner, back into the garage, and there was Danny, with Tara.

He was holding a gun. A very big gun. Right in her face.

You know a lot of people up here have guns in their houses for hunting or whatever, but my parents weren't those people. I didn't know anything about guns, and that one scared the shit out of me. I had read stories in *News/North* about women being abused by their partners and one time there had been a hostage-taking downtown because some guy was mad at his wife but it wasn't something I had ever really seen, or understood.

Danny was a little guy; he really wasn't any bigger than I was. He was facing towards me, and Tara was still sitting on the cooler just in front of me. I truly could look down the barrel of that gun. I will always remember that. I know now that it was an old shotgun, but then, all I knew was that guns could kill, and that I had left Tara to die when Flat Richard had asked me to take care of her.

Maybe part of what I did next can be explained by telling you how I felt about Danny Pond. He'd been teasing me for years in horrible nasty ways that I still can't explain why I had accepted. He regularly undid my bra in science class. He pinched me, pulled me, groped me, and then called me things like ugly and frigid. I never told on him, but I couldn't understand why beautiful girls like Tara regularly continued to go for him and basically give him what he wanted.

At first, for what felt like a long time, I was mesmerized by the view down the barrel … but then he grunted or something, and I looked up into his eyes. I guess I could see that there wasn't much there, because then I lashed out. I came at him right over top of Tara, knocking her down to one side of the cooler, and took the barrel of the gun in one hand as my other hand reached out at his throat. I knocked him down to the dirty concrete floor of the garage and straddled him, pinning his arms to his sides. I raised the gun above my head and was about to slam the butt down at him, when Tara grabbed me from the back.

"Doooon't hhuurrt him! I looove him you bitch" she shrieked, pulling me backwards by the hair. All I was worried about was that stupid fucking gun. I had never even had one in my hands before, and I was worried that it might go off. I must have looked ridiculous, because I grabbed it like it was a can of pop that might overflow, and put my thumb over the mouth.

"You idiot, he had a gun to your head." I muttered at her through gritted teeth, trying with one leg to keep myself between them.

"It's only a duck rifle!" he said, still on the floor. "What the fuck are you, afraid of a duck rifle? Narc, you really don't have a clue." That was all I could take.

"Only a duck rifle, huh? Not scary at all, huh?" I took my thumb off the mouth, and lowered it back into his face. "Get the fuck out of here. GET THE FUCK OUT OF HERE." He pulled himself up off the ground. Tara couldn't seem to decide whether to help him or not.

"Bits—you wouldn't hurt anyone, right?" he asked slowly. I kicked him in the kneecap and he fell back down on his knees.

"I mean it. Get the fuck out of here."

He half crawled, half limped towards the outside door of the garage. Just as he reached it, Richard came through with Tara's older brother Keith. They looked at Danny, then over at me, uncertainly pointing the gun at him.

"Jesus. Bits."

Danny walked right past them out the door. Keith shook his head at his sister, then flipped her over one shoulder like a sack of potatoes.

"Can I put her in one of the rooms upstairs, Flat? Mom isn't gonna let her in the house like this." Richard nodded and we all headed back into the main part of the house.

Inside the house, nobody had noticed anything out of place. I was shaking, like I had just run a marathon, or been in an accident. I had just witnessed the greatest drama of my life to date, but it didn't seem to have registered with anyone there.

"BITS!" Jess appeared on the staircase. "You'll never believe what Missy just did…" She grabbed my hand and started pulling me toward the kitchen. I felt sick. I didn't want to be in a place where what I had just witnessed was a non-event. I couldn't remember why I had wanted to come, or what I had thought would happen. Then, another hand caught me from behind. I was scared for a moment, but then I looked back. It was Flat Richard, with his big, beautiful bear head looking at me like maybe he understood what I was feeling. He didn't say anything just then, but pulled me into a tight hug.

SHAWN MCCANN, author of *The Long Gun*, is a lifetime resident of Yellowknife. She is married with two children that both have a lot of exciting stories to tell. The vast majority of Shawn's writing experience is around writing speaking notes and government plans, but she annually engages in writing for fun during the Northwords Festival, and she does try to write at least one short story each year, and hopes to have  a novel drafted by 2035. It is always very exciting for Shawn to write without using acronyms. *The Long Gun* is Shawn's first published fiction.

Nonfiction

Lost

by AmberLee Kolson

There was no doubt about it. I was lost. I set my cranberry pail down on the leaf-strewn earth and scraped a rain-drizzled lock of hair from my face. I strained to hear a sound, any sound, other than the wind whirring past my ears in strong, uneven gusts. I was standing ankle deep in crunchy wet lichen and surrounded by scraggly fir trees, and the Ingraham Trail, half an hour out of Yellowknife, was nowhere to be seen.

Fighting back a rising wave of panic, I pushed back the wet sleeve of my oversized military jacket and checked my watch. It was four thirty, plenty of time to walk out of the bush and to the car, parked in a convenient roadside turnout, before dark. My heart sank as I pictured my backpack lying on the front seat of the car. It contained all of the necessities one might need if stranded: one litre of water, energy bars, a lighter, a Swiss army knife, rain cape, space blanket and water purifying tablets.

I clapped a hand on the left breast pocket of the jacket, suddenly remembering a toothpick container of matches I had carried, just in case, for the thirty years I had owned the coat. Feeling them under the fabric, solid and real, caused me to take heart. How had this happened, I asked myself as I peered through the mist shrouded trees. Even before that thought had flown I knew the answer.

Two hours earlier I had waded through a tangled mess of boreal underbrush in an attempt to find the elusive motherlode of cranberries, the sweet spot. It was an area so loaded down with fat, shiny, blood-red berries, hanging innocently in groups of six or more on thread-thin stems only inches apart, that a scream of delight was mandatory, as was dropping to one's knees to start picking. My four-litre plastic ice cream pail was full, testimony to the surplus I had found.

However, in the concentration required to follow the hoard, profuse under spindly skeletons of long-dead birch and fir, lush in rocky crevices of Precambrian outcrops and splashed dramatically across white lichen nestled under sumac bushes, I had forgotten to keep the road in sight, or at least within hearing. I had gotten turned around, and as a result, was now lost.

My heart thumped in my chest as I thought of another cardinal rule I had ignored. I had told no one where I was going and so neither of my sisters, whom I had come to Yellowknife to visit and bond with over forays into the bush to pick the autumn berry, knew where I was. Work commitments had claimed their days, and I was left to my own devices. It had been a spur of the moment decision to drive out to our preferred spot and scout out a good patch.

"HELLO!" I yelled into the wind. "HELLO!"

The silence that greeted me sent a shiver of fear coursing through me. I screamed and scrambled out of the bog faster than a mad bee zooming in on a target, and clambered up a sharp and slippery incline on hands and knees, my bucket bumping thickly against the exposed granite. At the top of the very high rise I turned around and around in horrified wonder at the sight before me. As far as the eye could see was a carpet of trees, mostly green but interspersed here and there with yellow and orange.

Powerless to stop the tears that began rolling down my cheeks, I stood perfectly still and watched as rain began to fall lightly, innocent enough, until the wind caught it and sent it pelting sharply across my body in uneven sheets. It grazed my face and intermingled with the moisture already present. I resisted the overpowering urge to give in to the bubbling hysteria and I counselled myself to remain calm. All would be lost if I did not keep my head.

Heart pounding and carefully measuring the heavy breaths inhaled through my nose and expelled through my mouth, an exercise calculated to calm and control, I crouched on my haunches and slid down the rock face into a thicket of brittle bushes covered in faded, nondescript foliage. From my previous elevated vantage point it had seemed that there was a clearing and a distinct path through the collar of trees that circled my hill.

There was not. A smaller but similar lichen-covered rocky area was surrounded by a scraggly fringe of the stunted but prolific fir tree. It was a pattern repeated dozens of times as I searched for a way out of the maze. Retracing my steps, turning and walking in the opposite direction, and imagining that I saw a path through the confusion of branches that I pushed my way through was an uninspired strategy. The only constant was a lake or large slough that I kept coming round to. It was clear that I was walking in circles.

It was also clear that night was falling. The rain and wind had died down. The clouds had rolled away, leaving a black sky where no stars twinkled to brighten the dusk that surrounded me. It was cold too. I shivered. It was more the fear of knowing I would be spending at least one night on the land than from a lack of warmth.

In an unexpected turn of good luck I happened upon a very large rocky knoll with two fir trees growing close together at the very peak. It struck me that I would be safer on higher ground, and the trunks and upper branches were tailor-made for a lean-to. In the gloom I gathered deadfall and hauled it to the spot. As I was placing the wood to form my open-air fort, a crashing in the underbrush told me I was not alone.

Preoccupied with finding a path out of the bush, I had not thought about wild animals until that moment. It was dark. I was petrified. I tried to make out what the animal might be while planning a line of defense. From the shape I concluded that it was a bear. But it did not act like a bear. Or did it? It sat down about twenty feet from me and didn't move. Fortunately I knew what to do with bears.

I started screaming. The bear would be frightened by my piercing shrieks and amble off. From what I had read, bears were not confrontational and shunned contact with humans. My bear was different. It sat, immobile. With its poor eyesight perhaps it was trying to discern how much of a threat I was. Or maybe it was hoping that if it sat quietly I would go away.

The bear remained eerily still. I lowered my voice and began speaking to it in a conversational manner, explaining why it should turn around and retreat. All entreaties fell on deaf ears. Unlike the bear, I could not remain still and began to pile sticks, logs and chunks of lichen on the back wall of the shelter in the hopes of dispelling an overabundance of nervous energy. At some point, while keeping an eye on the bear as I worked, I began singing.

"I shot the sheriff, but I did not shoot the deputy." It was the only song that came to mind. It served me well that night. Checking over my shoulder to make sure the bear was still glued to his spot, I found he had gone. Critics. I quickly overlaid any remaining branches on the lean-to and finished it, giddy with relief.

It had cooled off considerably and I was chilled in my damp clothing. A fire would ward off the cold and create a line of defense between potential animal attackers and me. This next task did not go well. The wood was wet, as were the tissues and paper towels in my coat pocket. Nevertheless, I arranged a small grouping of twigs, paper and lichen shreds on a rock and pulled out the match container. One by one I tried all twenty-two, to no avail. The sulphur had disintegrated. The matches were useless.

What now? I stood at the entrance of the lean-to and looked up. A sheet of flawless sapphire, highlighted in dramatic fashion by feathery silhouettes of the ever-present fir trees, provided the perfect showcase for millions of twinkling diamond stars. It was breathtakingly beautiful. It was also profoundly silent. Looking at my watch by the light of the gigantic rising moon I saw it was ten o'clock. Nine hours until morning.

I checked the time five minutes later, and a couple of minutes after that. At ten fifteen precisely I heard a sound. It was so far in the distance that I could barely make it out. It seemed a very good possibility that my ears were playing tricks on me because I thought I heard a dog barking. It continued long enough for me to positively identify it and then it stopped.

I decided there and then that if it began to bark again that would be a sign. I would follow the sound in a straight line. If the dog stopped barking I would stop. When it barked again I would walk some more. The dog had been provided as salvation for me if I had the courage to accept the challenge. It began to bark, and faint with fear, I picked up my cranberry pail and a long sturdy stick and began to feel my way over the rock. I slipped and rolled down the hill and into a marsh of muskeg.

It was soft. It was fragrant. It was also very wet. Ice water oozed through my clothing, chilling me instantly. I picked myself up and listened for the dog as I sank knee deep into the bog. Water seeped into my shoes and when I tried to walk one of them was sucked off my foot. I considered leaving it. As I reached down the hole to retrieve it I heard the dog again take up its grievance with the world.

Proceeding resolutely in its direction, I stumbled through dense boreal forest, branches whipping me in the face, deadfall stabbing my legs, and an uneven floor constantly tripping me up. After forcing my way through a large burned-out area, I came to another muskeg marsh. Directly across from it stood a massive black wall of rock.

Exhausted, I began to cry.

"Help me," I prayed.

There had been no canine assistance for some time. I had been walking in what I hoped was the right direction. At that moment I felt the very strong presence of my grandmother, a native elder. It was positive, encouraging energy, and as I turned back to the embankment a pink phosphorescent spritz of fairy dust dropped to the ground ahead of me. I was being shown the way.

I scaled the large boulders and stood on level ground. Another pink neon spritz fell about twenty feet to my left. Accepting the gift that had been given to me I followed the luminous dissolving sprinkles until they delivered me to a sandy path bordered on both sides with glowing green lichen, guiding runway lights. Which way should I go?

With some trepidation I turned left, toward what looked like, in the distance, alien spaceships landing. Glowing lemon-coloured orbs appeared in the sky and settled gently to earth, disappearing from sight. I was undecided as to whether I would rather be lost forever or be taken up to another world. As I advanced toward the unearthly vision my fanciful imaginings were set to rest.

I was witnessing the headlights of cars as they crested a hill and then descended down the other side. It was at this point, in the dark, that they resembled spaceships landing. I ran as best as I could along the trail so as to be as close as I could to the next passing vehicle. Almost immediately headlights appeared. I put my cranberry pail down and began waving my stick in hopes that the driver would see the movement through the trees and stop.

Two yellow lights swam towards me hazily, as if through a fog, zigzagging back and forth, in and out of my vision. I began to think my imagination had gone astray when all at once the lights rounded the last corner and I saw a truck bearing down on me at great speed. The driver hit the brakes and the truck screeched to a halt less than ten feet from where I was standing, right in the middle of the highway.

The driver leaned over the steering wheel and gaped at me in amazement. I watched in frozen silence as his expression changed from one of disbelief, to bewilderment, and then curiosity. He jumped out of his truck and stood on the road, his hands on his hips, a poor man's Superman.

"It's three o'clock in the morning! You scared the hell out of me! I almost ran you over! What are you doing out here at this hour?"

As I stood before my saviour, all fear, anxiety and tension drained out of me. I felt unbearably weak and the stick dropped from my hands. As I spoke a lively phosphorescent aurora borealis streaked across the sky, leaving in its wake a sprinkling of glistening pink fairy dust.

"I was lost," I said.

AMBERLEE KOLSON, author of *Lost*, was born and raised in Yellowknife and is Métis, of Chipewyan and Polish descent. She holds a Bachelor of Education Degree in English from the University of Alberta and an Honors Culinary Arts Degree from Northern Alberta Institute of Technology. *Wings of Glass* (Theytus Books), her first novel, won the CBC Cross Country Bookshelf Contest for the north region  and a bronze medal in the 2011 Pub West book design award. AmberLee has completed *Cook Zilla*, a cooking mystery, and *Land's End*, a work of fiction.

Ts'ankui Theda, The Kindness of the Lake

by Brian Penney

Every year, my fishing buddy and I consider all the options in meticulous detail. We spend hours cruising the Internet, examining tour packages in Mexico, Brazil and South Africa. We discuss the details of each destination: the costs, the target species, the preferred season, the gear required, the amenities along the way. Then, at the last minute, like ten-year-old boys, we set all rational considerations aside to follow our stomachs and go fishing.

It is now the last minute. We must decide where to go. I am leafing through a pamphlet, Tuna Fishing In Belize, when the doorbell rings. It is my neighbour.

"What you are doing?" she says in greeting. She is positively glowing. "I have some fish for you!" She has just returned from her annual pilgrimage to visit Ts'ankui Theda, the Old Lady of the Falls. There she made her offerings, confessed her sins and received the blessings she sought, one of which must have been this fine fish.

It is not just any fish. It is a side of lake trout, lightly smoked over an open campfire. This lady is Denesoltine. She was brought up on fish. She has just returned from Tu Nedlé, the east arm of Great Slave Lake. This lady knows her fish. I cut a small slice across the grain. Its flesh is firm, red, and tasty.

"This is Kashé trout, the best!" she exclaims, enjoying the fish as much as I do. "We like the smaller ones, the females, like this… ten, twelve pounds. They have the best flavour."

These are the smaller ones?! The die is cast. We will fish in our own backyard. And what a backyard it is, with 1,500 miles of shoreline. We will leave early in the morning, sailing into the sun and following the eastern arm until it touches the coattails of Ts'ankui Theda. We know she bestows blessings on fishermen. Surely she will grant us a few of her fine fish.

Aside from being one of its largest lakes, the Great Slave Lake is also the deepest in North America. Westerly winds can create dangerous conditions, with waves of over thirty feet. The weather can change quickly and dramatically. There are few secure anchorages and its shoreline is dominated by high cliffs. We will have several hundreds of miles to go in an open, twenty-foot boat. All I need do now is tell my fishing buddy.

"The East Arm?" Joe says, a twinkle in his eye. "Excellent! The Newfies are heading out that way, too!"

For the last four months, Joe has been working for a construction crew consisting mostly of itinerant Newfoundlanders. This is the perfect opportunity to go "one-up" on them. He has heard stories of the East Arm, stories of humungous lunkers weighing over sixty pounds. Joe is a trophy hunter.

"That's a long ways," he adds. "How much gas are we gonna need?"

"Well, you can never have too much gas," I reply. Gas is his responsibility.

In fact, almost everything is his responsibility. My sole domains are the boat and a satellite telephone in case we become marooned. Joe takes care of everything else: a tent, camping gear, eating utensils, camp stove, food, etc. But all of his equipment is at home, on Vancouver Island. With two days before we leave, it will be a wild scramble as he tests the newfound friendships he has made in Yellowknife.

He calls from work the following day. The Newfoundlanders say a store in town is selling ciscoes. Since he cannot get away from work, he asks me to pick some up. If I am not quick, the Newfies will scoop up all the bait. When I arrive at the store, there is only one pack of ciscoes left.

As for the satellite telephone, I have mixed feelings. Certainly, with a small, open boat, there is a legitimate risk that we could be weathered in, unable to travel. The government advises all boaters in the area to submit a plan to the authorities before venturing into the eastern arm. This is only common sense. Still, there is something within me that resists. I tell my dear wife not to worry, not to phone Search and Rescue, that we shall return however long it takes.

On the day of our departure, we are ill prepared. We rush about from house to house, gathering miscellaneous gear borrowed from friends—a net here, a fishing rod there and so on. We have no time to check the weather forecast. By the time we are prepared to cast off, the sun is high in the sky.

On one count, Joe is very well prepared. He has a cooler filled with beer on ice, as well as an expansive collection of hard liquor—vodka, whisky, rum, tequila. If we are marooned on a far-flung shore, we will not abide in sobriety. The government is also very clear on this subject. One is not permitted to operate a marine vessel under the influence. This is common sense. What is it about people? They know better than to drink and drive but on the water, they will drink until they are loaded to the gunnels.

Leaving Yellowknife, we are greeted by high winds. We put the bow to the waves, an eight-foot swell with ten-foot peaks. There is only one speed—full throttle. We surf the crests of the waves, occasionally falling into a trough, slamming down with a thud that rattles our bones. We are drenched in no time. We don our rain gear on the fly.

I am rebalancing the load when we hit just such a trough. Vaulting forward, my head hits the windshield with a thud, splitting my cheek. Now I remember the first aid kit! I hold an oily rag to my face until the bleeding stops. As we round the cape off Yellowknife Bay, the weather only gets worse. There are dark clouds on the horizon, the distant rumble of thunder in our ears.

"C'mon," I bellow skyward, springing to my feet, clutching the windshield, "Is that the best you can do? You call this a storm?" This is when I notice that I've lost my life jacket, which, of course, I had been using as a seat cushion.

All the same, we retreat to the protection of outlying islands, clinging to the shore of the great lake as a child would cling to his mother's skirt. Here the chop recedes to a more manageable height. After a time, we find ourselves in calm, fishable waters. We cannot resist.

Fish on! This one fights the noble fight. As I reel him in, Joe is on hand with the net. The fish jumps straight through it! The net has a gaping hole. Still, the fish remains tethered to the line. We haul him aboard.

"Slough shark!" Joe yells. The northern pike, a boney, ugly alligator of a fish, is exactly the fish we wished to avoid. We have become purist, seeking only lake trout. Still, as we toss him back, I wonder if we should have kept him in case our supplies run out.

We continue east as I mend the net. The sky has fallen into the sea and dark clouds muster about us. When we leave the protection of the outlying islands, the winds pick up. Whitecaps thunder over the bow. I spend the next hour bailing water until we reach the shelter of another island.

"This is hard on gas," Joe observes.

"She's a regular gas pig," I say, referring to the ninety horsepower two-stroke.

We pull into a secluded cove with an abundant supply of driftwood. Here we will stop for a mug-up. As I tie on, Joe grabs a jerry can of gas and heads for the pile of driftwood. It is a colossal pile, at least fifty cords. There is no need to instruct Joe. Early in life he attained the rank of Eagle Scout.

"You can never have too much gas," I yell to him.

He douses the wood. Then whoooossshhh! The flames are dancing high above his head. The fire crackles and pops, leaping skyward. The heat is intense. Joe retreats to the boat where, with a half-pound of butter, fresh mushrooms and steak, he cooks supper over a camp stove. We have only one fork, which we share.

"You can't do that in British Columbia," he says, admiring his handiwork.

Yes, it is a campfire that you could see from outer space. And how many times in a lifetime does one have a chance to do something that can be seen from outer space? The government has guidelines concerning campfires. I could recite them to Joe but, honestly, they only amount to common sense.

It is twilight by the time we leave the secluded cove. At this time of year, in the land of the midnight sun, that means about eleven o'clock. Despite low visibility, we soldier on, clinging to the north shore of the lake. Eventually, we find a string of buoys to guide our passage.

Before long, it is pitch black. We can no longer discern the yonder shore. The high winds have abated. Joe ties us on to a buoy. This practice is sternly discouraged by the Canadian Coast Guard and marine authorities everywhere, as is the consumption of alcoholic beverages on marine vessels. We are lulled into a sense of false security as the wind dies. We drink Black Russians. Slowly, we are enveloped in peace and quiet.

As I slumber, I dream of Ts'ankui Theda, the Old Lady of the Falls. Hers is a story that has been told a thousand times in a thousand different voices. But the essentials remain. As a young girl, her people feasted on beaver. She wanted only a cupful of blood but their leader told her this was not for her. She did not protest. She remained seated where she was well after her people had moved on.

When they noticed her absence, they sent a runner back to retrieve her. They were, after all, heading for the great barren lands, the Land of Little Sticks, where there would be caribou meat for all. She replied that, though she wanted to join them, she could no longer move. She would stay as she was, seated beneath the falls.

Having little knowledge of the Dene and their medicine people, I do not know exactly what to make of her story. You could say she was hard done by but for some reason she decided to repay their unkindness with generosity. In any case, generations of Dene have made offerings to her. In return, their wishes come true, whether it is health, food or long life that they seek.

As I sleep, the boat rocks like a cradle. It is gentle and hypnotic, the waves lapping against the gunnels. It feels like a cradle rocked by the hand of Ts'ankui Theda herself. Gradually I realize we are in motion. We are adrift!

"Joe," I yell, springing to my feet, "Joe!" He is dead to the world, sleeping soundly in the bow. So I kick him hard in the ribs.

"We're adrift, you scurvy dog!" I yell. "Man the helm!"

To his credit, he springs into action, starts the engine and puts the bow to the wind. Now we are bobbing on the waves in pitch black. There is neither sight nor sound of the shore. I search, in the darkness, for the buoy. I wonder what sort of knot this Eagle Scout had used to tie us on. There is no need to go anywhere. We have no idea where we are.

"I'm sure I tied us off proper and secure," he mumbles.

"Maybe that's the problem." I reply. "Perhaps you should have tied us on instead."

"Oh well," he says with a sigh, "at least we have the satphone. We can give them a call and get our position."

"We don't need any of that crap," I say. Hmmm, why didn't I rent a satphone or a GPS? Why didn't I at least bring a map?

We maintain our position, the motor idling, waiting for a change of weather. The water here is murky and deep, over 700 feet according to the fish finder. Ever so slowly, the sun rises behind dark clouds. A gentle wind parts the sky. Still, there is no sight of land as we wait an hour, two hours.

"This is hard on the gas," Joe observes.

"Yeah, you can never have too much gas," I reply.

Then, as I am resting, lying back gazing skyward and sipping my morning beer, I see an eagle soaring high above us.

"That way!" I shout triumphantly. We follow the eagle, who takes us to a high cliff, its red granite glowing in the sun. At the foot of the cliff, seagulls are feasting on ciscoes. Where there are little fish, there are big fish. At long last, we are baiting our lines.

Tradition, many will argue, is sometimes a barrier to success. That may be so. Still, I cut up a couple of ciscoes to chum the waters. Now we have only three left for bait. To his credit, Joe keeps his mouth shut. Still, I can hear his teeth grinding.

He is busy baiting his hook, slipping a cisco into its harness. I notice he is using the same knot I use, a palomar, which is a simple double loop. It is a good choice for me, for I have braided line, thirty-pound test. On the other hand, he is using monofilament, twenty-pound test. It is not such a good choice for him. To my credit, I keep my mouth shut.

With his first cast, his line snaps tight. He has hooked into a big one. I reel in to give them room to play. I rush to the gunnels with the net to see a fantastic trout, twenty or thirty pounds, slowly rising from the deep. Suddenly, he breaks the surface, so near we could touch him, leaps in a violent arc and breaks the line.

"Son of a bitch!" Joe exclaims. "This line is old and brittle." He snaps it with his hands by way of demonstration. I guess he borrowed this gear from the wrong person.

Now he is rummaging through his tackle box, looking for something he knows is not there—extra line. To ask me for line will irritate him to no end. So I offer him a spool of thirty-pound test. It is not that I don't want to irritate him. It is simply that this sort of irritation does not meet my standards; it is not sufficiently subtle. I take another tack as he spools the line onto his reel.

"There's two hundred yards on that spool," I say.

"I know," says Joe. He hates being told anything.

"How do you know?" I ask.

"'Cause it says so on the spool."

"No, it doesn't," I reply. "It says three hundred yards on the spool. I took a hundred yards off."

"Yeah, like I said, two hundred yards!"

With that, he cast his line again. As we troll, we discover an under-water ledge. The fish finder beeps like Morse code. The water is filled with fish at depths ranging from thirty to one hundred feet. We have no weights so we tie nuts and bolts to our lines. At last we have found the honey hole of our dreams but, for bait, we have only two ciscoes.

Another strike! This time, his line holds. We pull a lunker over the side that Joe promptly weighs. The scale reads exactly eighteen pounds. "A twenty-five pounder!" I yell. That's fishing for you; it makes boys of men.

We split the fish to examine the liver and heart. This is a healthy female, rich with eggs. In its stomach, we find a half-dozen ciscoes intact, just like they had come from a store. We let the seagulls fight over the remains.

We are in seventh heaven. We have an ample supply of bait, clear cold waters and an eagle perched high above us, our guardian. We are ten years old again. With every second cast, we hook into these fine Kashé trout. Joe turns off the fish finder. Its incessant beeping has become repetitive and irritating. We know they are here en masse, glutting themselves on cisco.

The government has regulations in place to preserve fish stocks. This is "catch-and-release" country. The catch limit is one trout per person. The possession limit is two. We are born free, yet everywhere we are in shackles. We fish until our hearts are content.

By now the hour is late. We do not have another night to spend on the lake. Our supply of gas is perilously low. Still we are not far from Parry Falls, the home of the Ts'ankui Theda. Beyond the next cape, I am certain we will find the Lockhart River, the river that flows from heaven. But we are not looking for God. We have come for fish. Instead, I sprinkle a pinch of tobacco on the water, a silent offering to the Old Lady of the Falls. Goodbye and thanks for all the fish!

We decide, reluctantly, to return to civilization. It is a bone-crushing ride at high speed. But, when one is returning home with a bounti-ful catch, time and trouble are like water off a duck's back. Being low on gas, we skirt the reefs and shoals on the landward side of the buoys. In a truly unbelievable stroke of luck, we find the life jacket we lost two days ago. We are blessed. At the wharf, a stranger asks about our catch.

Joe is ebullient, effusive in his description of the bounty we have found. This, from my point of view, is a major faux pas. In my tradition, we always deny that we have caught any fish whatever. At least Joe does not tell the truth about where we have been. In fact his story bears no relationship to the facts whatever, consisting mostly of the forty and fifty pounders we were obliged to release.

My neighbour is well pleased with my catch. She takes the heads, a delicacy amongst the Dene. She will boil them up, a feast for her family. Friends and family fill my home, dining on poached trout, trout fried in butter and olive oil, trout baked in a secret family recipe of herbs and spices. The good friends who lent us the holey net and the brittle line also share the bounty of T'ankui Theda.

As for Joe, he gives the camp cook enough fish for the whole crew. His delight is doubled by the fact that the Newfoundlanders have not caught even one slough shark. They are extremely grateful, for trout is a delicacy amongst these people as well. But when the fish is gone, surely they will resent him for succeeding where they have failed.

Amongst Newfoundlanders, fishing is bred in the bone. They sense, deep within their being, a fundamental shift in the order of things. They have been out-fished by a Canadian. This cannot stand. They immediately press him for details.

"Where'd ya go to, b'y? If ya tell's us where they're to, we can go where they's at."

To his credit, Joe's answers are vague, almost meaningless. He did not catch the trophy he sought. He found something far more valuable: the grudging esteem of other fishermen.

"Youse come wit us, b'y. We's will get the gas. How much gas is we gonna need?" they ask.

"Arrr, you can never have too much gas," Joe replies.

He politely declines their offer. He tells me that the Newfound-landers will re-double their efforts next weekend. They will send four boats to the East Arm in search of the elusive lake trout. If fortune smiles upon them, they will discover for themselves the kindness of the lake. Surely this is as it should be.

BRIAN PENNEY, author of *Ts'sankui Theda, The Kindness of the Lake*, is a sports fisherman who works in his free time as a management consultant. His other interests include biking, blues and Buddhism. *Ts'sankui Theda, The Kindness of the Lake* is Brian's first published story.

Beauty of the Butte

by Karen McColl

S cott slowed his pace until his steps were almost synchronized with my short gait. Our eyes met. "It's pretty special, isn't it?" he said.

I just smiled: the landscape could speak for itself. A cool but light breeze danced around our shirts as we crunched over the dry tundra en route to the summit. Walking delicately to avoid crushing early spring flowers, I scanned our surroundings. Below us, the Liard River dissected a smooth carpet of boreal forest stretching out beyond the horizon. On the other side of the Nahanni and Liard Mountain Ranges, the South Nahanni River snaked its way lazily across the wide valley it carved millions of years ago. Hiking under blue skies with hours of daylight left to savour, it was definitely a moment closing in on perfection.

A hike up the Butte is an incredible yet little-known experience, because like most mountains in the Northwest Territories, it isn't the easiest place to access. Known in Slavey Dene as Tthenáágó, meaning strong rock, the Butte spreads up from a solitary ridge across the South Nahanni River from the tiny Dene village of Nahanni Butte. Sitting near the confluence of the Liard River, "the Butte" is an affectionate name for both this village of one hundred and twenty residents and the opposing 1,217-metre high mountain.

Although close to six hundred potential hikers pass below this unassuming mountain every summer at the tail end of a canoe or raft trip on the South Nahanni River, few people take the opportunity to hike it. There are a number of reasons for this. One is relativity. By the time paddlers arrive at Nahanni Butte, they have already spent a week or more surrounded by a landscape so magnificent that it regularly graces the pages of international magazines. Although it makes a beautiful backdrop for pictures, Tthenáágó doesn't immediately stand out next to the one hundred mountains upriver. Also, because people often end their trip at Nahanni Butte by hiring a water-taxi to return to their parked vehicles, having a shower and a restaurant meal become higher priorities than hiking a mountain.

Another reason for the low hiking numbers is the bugs. As long-time Nahanni River outfitter Neil Hartling stated in his 1993 book on the area: "Three things are certain in life: taxes, death and mosquitoes in Nahanni Butte." While locally produced T-shirts depicting the "Nahanni Butte mosquito dance," make light of the situation, the reality is that mosquitoes are no laughing matter for most people, especially at the rate they flourish in Nahanni Butte.

Descending the South Nahanni River is not the only way of reaching Tthenáágó; it can also be ascended. Since Nahanni Butte is only boat or aircraft accessible in the summer, the shortest option to access Tthenáágó is to paddle eleven kilometres down the Liard River from the Nahanni Butte access road and then a short distance *up* the South Nahanni River. Although not overly difficult, it does require a bit of foresight and planning, as well as a sense of adventure.

Tthenáágó therefore remains a relatively lonely peak, saving its magic almost exclusively for Nahanni "Butte-ers" and outdoor enthusiasts from nearby areas who are willing to put in a bit of effort.

My friend Mike, a young Butte-er of mixed descent from the aggressive Nahæa people who mysteriously disappeared from the Nahanni area more than a hundred years ago, says that most of Nahanni Butte's residents have been up Tthenáágó. He himself has been up three times, and someone told me once that another local made it to the summit in one hour, though the endeavour normally takes three to five hours with a light daypack.

Picturesque Tthenáágó had caught the attention of a couple of my friends during their work trips to the area, and when a hiking adventure was suggested, I jumped at it. I was hungry to get my mountain-high and feel the burn in my legs after a winter of cross-country skiing on the flats. Four of us—three men and I, the lone woman—discussed the logistics of our trip in my friend Scott's living room in Fort Simpson one day after work. By tackling the Butte in early June, we hoped to avoid the worst of mosquito season. Unlike South Nahanni River paddlers, we only needed a weekend to carry out our "trucks, canoes and hiking boots" adventure from Fort Simpson. Examining a Google Earth map, we estimated the upstream paddle on the South Nahanni River to be about three kilometres.

Although I had never paddled upstream before, I was drawn to the challenge. Local prospector Albert Faille and adventurer R.M. Patterson had canoed, poled and lined their way up the South Nahanni River several times in the late 1920s and thirties. Sometimes they had the help of a kicker (motor), but even if they did, it likely ran out of gas before reaching their destination at the Flat River or Virginia Falls. The Dene, with their thousands of years of experience in the area, were more likely to travel beside the river on foot or by dog team and descend the same way or by building a large boat made of several moose hides.

Bumping down the Liard highway in my friend Alex's sporty truck on a Friday evening after work, I could feel our shared excitement. Or perhaps it was just that I felt Alex's two big dogs—husky mutts of course—panting heavily behind me. I met Alex the previous summer when our dogs got into an awkward scrap that left us both running, leash in hand, in opposite directions. Luckily, our many impromptu encounters in the small produce section of the Northern Store had become our running joke and we had become fast friends. Alex was an affable character with a large social network, and one of his good friends was my co-worker, Scott, the brains behind this trip.

Scott was a level-headed project manager whose strength of character has more than once been mistaken for overt seriousness. Those who got close to him discovered the depth of his kindness and generosity, and I considered myself fortunate to have befriended him during our year working together. Two weeks earlier, during the May long weekend, we and four others had shared a frigid yet enjoyable paddling trip on the Kakisa River and Great Slave Lake.

Rounding out our group was a Fort Simpson local, Michael, who I had spent the least amount of time with but still knew well enough from Friday nights at the curling lounge. Although Michael was more of an acquaintance before this trip, his laid-back personality and quirky sense of humour quickly propelled him into the friend category. Both Michael and Scott had paddled the South Nahanni River several times as canoe guides, but had never hiked the Butte.

In my side mirror I watched Scott's red truck, with two canoes strapped onto a homemade two-by-four canoe rack, pull into the Nahanni Butte access road behind us. Shortly before reaching our planned first night destination, we spotted a black bear munching on some grass in the ditch. Alex and I had a clever idea. We opened the windows to let the dogs bark and scare the heck out of the bear to ensure it didn't bother us later. We were dismayed however, when TJ and Sadie whined like ninnies, evoking, so I imagined, nothing more than an eye-roll from the bear. The second black bear we saw, one hundred metres from camp, forced us into plan B. We would hit the river that night. Even if we had to camp in thick bush, it would be better than lying wide-awake in our tents all night, listening for the tell-tale twig-snapping sounds of an approaching animal.

It was after ten by the time we pushed our canoes off the shore and into the slow moving waters of the Liard. While I was secretly pleased that Michael had let me take first shift in the stern, I noticed that Scott and Alex, with the two big dogs, didn't look quite as relaxed. TJ, a one-hundred-pound beast, was throwing his weight this way and that, causing the canoe to lurch precariously with each movement. "Sit!" Alex commanded futilely several times, while Scott did his best to balance the canoe.

"Are you sure TJ doesn't belong in the Whitehorse Beringia Centre?" Scott quipped, referring to TJ's large prehistoric-sized head. Michael and I paddled on serenely, powerless to do anything other than watch in both sympathy and amusement as Alex and Scott prepared themselves for the possibility of a frigid late-evening swim.

Somehow we all managed to stay dry, and it wasn't long before we unexpectedly stumbled upon an idyllic island. The decision to camp was quick and unanimous and we drifted to shore, beckoned by the flat sand beach and pink sunset. I couldn't help thinking how perfect everything was as I unloaded our gear from the canoe and admired the beautifully calm and bug-free evening.

"Where's the three-person tent?" I asked Alex a few minutes later, when he started setting up his two-person tent. I was met with a blank stare and a furrowed brow.

"You're kidding me, right?" I asked incredulously.

Despite our five-minute group conversation at the parking lot deliberating over who would sleep with whom and in what tent, we had somehow forgotten the larger tent. And through all the confusion we didn't even know who was to blame.

The thought of four of us squeezing into a two-person tent was clearly ludicrous and totally hilarious, or at least I thought so. And since I was in such high spirits, it was voted that I paddle back upstream to the truck. Scott agreed to join me, although he didn't find the situation quite as humorous.

It was a slow paddle against the gentle current, but surprisingly enjoyable. It was my first spring in the north and the novelty of canoeing under the early morning glow so close to solstice did not escape me. The time was passed quickly with good conversation and in less than two hours we pulled back onto shore, tent in hand and welcomed by our smiling friends and the glow of a campfire. Exhausted but filled with the adrenaline of our unexpected adventure, we shared conversation over the fire for a short while until Alex broke the reverie.

"It's starting to get light out." I had just noticed the same thing. At 2:30 a.m., before the sky went fully dark, it was getting light again. Bedtime!

Coming Home

The next morning we were groggy but spirited as we munched on a breakfast of homemade bagels and jam, courtesy of Michael's wife Tracy. The almost cloudless sky boded well for summit day.

"I'm sorry for mouth-breathing all night, guys," I apologized to my tent partners, Michael and Scott, as I alternated between chewing and breathing. My head cold had amplified after an almost sleepless night.

"You are a bit of a snot-nose this morning," Alex remarked as I pulled yet another tissue out of my pocket. To my chagrin, this nickname stuck for the duration of the trip.

A relaxing paddle to the confluence, for Michael and me at least, was followed by an hour-long upstream grunt to get abreast of Nahanni Butte. There was no time for drinking water or nose scratching during this stretch—every missed stroke meant falling back a canoe length. It was a miniscule peek at what Faille and Patterson had endured for weeks on end! Finally we passed the village and rounded the rocky base of Tthenáágó.

According to the Dene, Tthenáágó is a giant beaver lodge. Their oral history tells of a family of giant beavers who were terrorizing the local Dene people by using their large tails to sink boats and kill people. Yamoria, a powerful medicine man, came to the aid of the people by hunting down the beavers. The beavers fled to their lodge at the top of Tthenáágó, but Yamoria got them out with a stick. He chased them to Trout Lake, where he killed one, and then far down the Mackenzie River where he killed the rest of them and stretched their pelts in the mountains near present-day Deline.

Wishing to be respectful of the traditional territory of the local Dene, we asked permission before coming to this area. Serendipitously, I had run into the chief, Fred Tesou, in Fort Simpson a couple of days before our trip. Offering my outstretched hand and introducing myself, I explained our plan.

"It's a great hike," he answered without hesitation. "You'll have a good time up there."

I was confident Fred was right, despite of a couple of minor hiccups. Such as not being able to find my only pair of hiking pants as I picked through my gear deciding what I would take up the mountain with me.

"Oh, the grey ones?" Alex asked when I enquired with the group. He was tying a red bandana over his shaved head. "Those were beside the empty barrel in the truck when we left."

That left me with three options, and paddling back to the truck for a second time was not one of them. I could hike in long underwear, rain pants, or shorts. Given the pleasant temperatures, I chose the latter, even though I knew the consequences.

Sporting our large overnight packs, we huffed our way up the first hill, one of the steepest sections of the hike, before stopping for lunch. Already grateful to take a break, I blew my nose and took a few healthy swigs from my water bottle. *Was I more out of shape than I realized?* It must just be the head cold, I reasoned.

The ramp soon narrowed and we gained the true ridge. Ridge hikes are my favourite because of the almost constant views—there is always something new to look at. The open cliff edge also provided a light breeze, keeping the mosquitoes at bay.

When we weren't walking on a precipitous edge, we were pushing headfirst through dwarf birch, spruce trees and rosebushes, which criss-crossed my pasty legs with red battle wounds with each step I took. While we encountered occasional flagging tape and faint traces of trail, the route up was mostly a bushwhack. Scott, the mountain goat, was usually leading, while Alex pulled up the rear with TJ and Sadie. Michael, who we joked looked like Mr. Peanut with his capped hat, hiking pole, and scrawny legs, floated somewhere in the middle with me. Once or twice, I tried cleverly to shortcut the route and sneak past Scott but I was always stymied and forced to catch up with my tail between my legs. I would have made a fine sled dog, always determined to catch the leader and never realizing the impossibility.

By five p.m. we reached a beautiful saddle at the treeline with our first views across the South Nahanni valley and Liard plain. Happily dropping our bags, we deliberated the next move.

With our water supplies running low, we opted for completing the hike that night rather than waiting for the following morning. We would have a late dinner and camp here tonight, then hike down to our canoe tomorrow. Combining our essentials into one backpack, we set off into the alpine. Scott took the first turn with the backpack, which unfortunately didn't slow him down any. Still, I felt wonderful and weightless as we scrambled over large rocky areas and zigzagged our way up the ridgeline.

Not long after conquering the steepest part, large rocks and scree started to fade into dry shrubs and the occasional snow patch. Pausing to scoop snow into our water bottles, we admired a group of violet-green tree swallows dipping and diving above us like synchronised swimmers.

We soon crested the flat-topped peak area, leaving only rolling terrain between us and the true summit. My competitive streak forgotten, I allowed myself to slow down and fall behind the others. Gone were the brambles and bushes grabbing at my legs, urging me to hurry up. Taking my time to absorb my surroundings, I snapped photos and crouched to examine some of the hardy spring flowers that dotted the tundra like proud soldiers.

It was there that Scott joined me. After a few moments of walking together in silent appreciation, I exploded with enthusiasm. "This is *amazing*! I had no idea it would be so cool! I'm really glad we came here."

"Pretty cool, hey snot-nose!" Alex chimed in from a few metres away.

"Yeah, I can't believe I've never been up here before!" Michael added, leaning on his hiking pole with outstretched arms.

We reached the summit by seven p.m., marked by an old fire tower and radio repeater. We took our time here, soaking in the 360 degree view and taking the kind of pictures I was sure would one day grace the pages of NWT tourism advertisements. It was truly one of the most spectacular vistas I had ever set my eyes upon, made better still with the knowledge that relatively few people had the opportunity to get here.

Pondering the power of this special place, I thought back to something I had read recently about an older Dene man who acknowledged that he didn't understand why anyone would hike a mountain if they weren't hunting. This is a very practical consideration from the point of view of someone living on the land. I agree—hiking is strenuous, time-consuming and frivolous. But everything is relative and hiking, to me, is a way to connect with nature. And Tthenáágó is a very special place. Looking upon the vast and extraordinary landscape with the wind whipping around me was a humbling and invigorating experience. And it made all the sweat, scratches and grime worth it, just like it does every time.

Mahsi cho Tthenáágó!

KAREN McCOLL, author of *Beauty of the Butte*, began freelance writing while living in the mountain town of Revelstoke, BC, squeezing in the odd feature or news story in between skiing, mountain-biking and camping. Her passion is for anything outdoors but she also loves writing about community events and cultural activities. Her move to Fort Simpson, NWT, in the spring of 2010 gave her new inspiration for writing about the people and places of the north. Although the Northwest Territories stole her heart, Karen's work with Parks Canada has temporarily taken her to Iqaluit, Nunavut. She misses trees, but is enjoying the adventure and figures that Yellowknife will feel like a tropical oasis after a winter spent on Baffin Island.

For Us

by January Go

It begins one winter morning in February with a fight. The sky is black. After so many long dark sleepless nights, my husband in his blue, thick robe wakes me. "Get up," he says. "It's 6:30. You have to prepare the children's lunches."

"Okay," I sigh. An hour passes.

"Get up. You still haven't made lunch."

"Oh my God! Why didn't you make it yourself?" I rush to the kitchen and quickly prepare deli sandwiches and put aside my anger with everything I hold dear.

"You know it's your turn to make lunch," my husband says. "What's wrong with you?"

"What is wrong with me? I cannot believe you are asking me this question."

"I hate it when you're like this. You're dragging me down."

"What? Excuse me for being so tired." I am now wrapping the fourth and last sandwich.

"You know what? I can't discuss this with you right now. I am going back to bed to get some sleep."

I lie down and cry. After all I sacrificed he tells me that I am dragging him down? I left my job so he could have the job that he wanted. I am far away from my mother and my sister, here with no friends, stuck at home because I have nowhere to go and because it is freezing outside. I am trying so hard to live this lifestyle, to live in Yellowknife—this isolated, strange place. Why should I continue to stay here when he is angry with me? The only reason I am in this forsaken place is him. Why does he not see that? My pillow is soaking wet with tears. He knocks on the door and says, "We're leaving now."

Careful for him not to notice my crying I almost choke when I say *Bye*.

That night he sleeps. And like the nights before this, I lie in bed unable to close my eyes, and even when I do, I stay awake. I find it hard to breathe. I am so tense my lungs are not functioning properly. I stand up and get out of bed, walk to the kitchen, and find myself opening a bottle of red wine. I finish the bottle while taking a thirty-minute soak in the bathtub.

Now here I am lying on the black leather couch that we bought at a bargain price from *YKTrader*. I smell so nice because of my vanilla-infused bath routine. My long black hair is flowing down the armrest. My legs rest on the back. My pink lace baby doll dress shows my silky undergarments. I am thinking of random questions that were asked of me twice, in completely different circumstances, by two different men. "How are you? Are you good? Are you happy? Is your husband treating you well?" What kind of questions were these? What was I supposed to say? I refused to answer the questions. And now I would be afraid to answer them.

I already know it is going to be my fault. I will feel the blame if things do not turn out well in this family. It will be me who ruins the dreams of a happy family. I am the person who is weak, the one who will tear this family apart. And I do not want to be that person. I have to pull myself together, work harder on keeping myself sane, and win this battle against myself. I think of having a discussion with my husband to find out whether he sees a future for us living somewhere else, like California, where there are big shopping malls, a variety of restaurants, where the options for filling every need and want are vast and great, where it is not extremely cold, where the sun rises and sets at a normal time, a place that is not isolated.

I think of making a big deal if he says no to relocating, that I will hold it against him for being selfish. I imagine us fighting, bickering at each other for petty things, screaming, nagging, not seeing eye to eye, slowly drifting apart, no longer making love. I see him burying himself in work so as not to think of me, playing too many video games, avoiding conversations with me. I see myself drowning in tears, turning to alcohol to ease the pain, taking sleeping pills so I get rest. I see myself scolding my children, screaming at them for tiny mistakes, unkind with my words, cold, unaffectionate, a distant mother. I think of myself leaving and never coming back.

The wine helped. I am now feeling a little sleepy, my muscles relaxed. I walk quietly to the bedroom, slowly creep to bed, and close my eyes as I surrender to wherever my thoughts lead me now.

It would be easy if my husband were a slob, chugging beer with a sagging beer belly, an insensitive brat, and a chauvinist pig. But he is not. He is the most loving, caring, kind, smart, charming man I have ever loved. Although he does not have a chiselled body, I am as attracted to him as the first time we became lovers, more than that actually. I love his slim build, his mocha skin, his broad shoulders, and most of all his arms. My heaven here on earth. I sleep in cloud nine when he wraps his arms around me and I lay my head on his chest, or just simply hug his arm like a full-size body pillow. I adore his sense of humour. He can make me laugh like no one else. It is orgasmic. He is intoxicating, and he makes me weak in the knees. He is my best friend, my own Prince Charming.

How stupid of me to think of leaving my husband who does not push me around, who treats me with affection and respect, who is not controlling, who does not care about unfolded clothes, a disorganized closet. He's a husband who cooks, gives our toddler a bath when I can't, a husband who washes dirty dishes. How unreasonable, selfish, inconsiderate, insensitive of me to be having these thoughts of leaving. How can I when every day I see him happy, eager to work and provide for his family, when he never ceases to kiss and hug me as he leaves for work and again as he gets home, when he makes a big breakfast of pancakes, bacon, and hash browns for us every Saturday morning? I know in my heart that no one else can satisfy me sexually, can nurture my need for laughter, that there is no one else I would rather hold hands with when I grow old.

Am I crazy? I think I am going crazy. Darn, I guess the wine was not enough. I toss and turn carefully so as not to wake him. I take my iPhone and browse Facebook, look at the news feeds and my photo albums. I look so different in photos that were taken just this past summer. I gained weight since the temperature dropped in October here in Yellowknife. I look awful. I feel awful. I feel that I have lost myself here. It is like I am not me anymore. I do not like looking in the mirror. This woman is dull, with drooping shoulders, very long tangled dry hair, and a colourless face. Her eyes are tired with big dark bags. She used to be polished and presentable but now she looks like a mess.

I was told that many people come to Yellowknife and stay for only a short period of time. Some leave because their work contract has ended, but a lot of people leave because they cannot stand winter. When my husband accepted his job here in Yellowknife a year ago, his co-workers were afraid that he might not survive the winter and that he would pack up and leave the job. He did not. I told my husband that Yellowknife felt like a place with a natural elimination process, whoever survives their first winter will stay for years. Those who do not, they never come back. It is as if Yellowknifers are a group of elite survivalists, and my husband is now one of them.

I am, however, still being tested. On *Oprah*, Iyanla Vanzant said, "If you don't have a test, you won't have a testimony." Well I don't think this testimony is going to be a good one. But is it really because of winter that I am feeling unhappy? Oh my God, I don't know anymore! My head hurts. I feel suffocated, choking. I am not expecting anyone to understand me because I do not understand myself. But here I am looking for answers as to what is wrong and why. This is killing me—to constantly tell myself that I can do this, that there is nothing wrong, that I should like it here.

Every night I stay awake because my mind won't instruct my body to relax, my lungs to breathe, my heart to calm, or my soul to clear. It won't tell me that there is nothing wrong here, that what is wrong is me. Do you know how hollow it feels to mentally beat yourself so hard because not a vein in your body will listen to how ridiculous you feel? And you fight this feeling, suppress it, bury it deep in your heart, careful with each word that comes out of your mouth because it could mean a revolution, and you already know that revolution will only lead to defeat. I am wrong to be feeling this way. It is my fault I am feeling trapped. This is how my life is going to be, for this is where I shall have to stay.

But is it wrong for me to choose to stay inside the house when it is freezing cold, even when what I really want to do is go out? Is it wrong for me to keep my sons warm inside because I do not want them to catch colds? Is it wrong for me to think that I have nowhere fun to go after visiting the small library? After spending time at a café with desserts that look like they were bought from a grocery store when all I want is a freshly baked cupcake? After walking through a mall that feels abandoned because of large empty spaces with CLOSED signs on the glass doors? After eating dull-tasting sushi at a restaurant and paying a high price for it when I know I could have amazing sushi at a fancy restaurant down south for the same price? Is it wrong for me to want something better, to yearn for more, to miss a lifestyle that I used to truly enjoy? Am I asking for too much? I feel so shallow.

My mother had warned me about this. She said that I should not leave my job for five years and move to Yellowknife for something uncertain. She knew Yellowknife would be different. "What if you don't like it there?" she said. I reasoned with her: "But I have no choice. I cannot have him working there while I work here and take care of our three children by myself. We have to be together. I don't want us living far away from each other."

Now I'm wondering if I made the right decision. I had a stable job and was working my way up, building a career. I remember feeling confused about the decision to come here but I knew I was doing it for my family. I remember being scared and not wanting to move but at the same time thinking that not wanting to move was selfish. Giving up all that I was used to in my daily life in exchange for a new life with my family being together was the hardest decision I have made. Someone said to me "It must be hard to be selfless." Being "selfless" was the easiest choice I had and the only one that made sense. I was asked if I had always been selfless to which I replied, "I just want things to be easier."

A friend of mine once told me that things happen for a reason. He said that this move was meant to happen because this is what I wanted, that I had wished in my mind and in my prayers for my family to be together and this was the answer to my wish. And now that the family is here I am still feeling confused, lost and depressed. Maybe I am having a mid-life crisis. Or maybe it is just the new environment and the new routine. The change from being a working mom with a hectic schedule to a house mom is shocking for my system. Maybe I am bored being a stay-at-home mother. Cooking, washing the dishes, doing the laundry, and keeping the house clean are not things that tickle my fancy. I can do them but I do not want to do them everyday. These tasks are tedious and repetitive. Some say that I should find something fun to do when I get bored, *Go out*. Yes, go out where? In the freezing cold? Frustrating.

At my previous work, this lady told me that when she stayed home with her first baby she was so bored she could not wait to go back to work. I miss work too. I miss being in the rush of meeting deadlines and schedules, seeing adults, being productive and earning my own money at the same time. I miss getting ready and dressing up for work. Now that I am a stay-at-home mom, I feel less valuable. I know it is wrong to feel this way because I have heard from so many people that being a mother is the most sacred job in the world and that it's fulfilling.

Leaving my job felt like a part of me was taken away. I do not know who I am anymore, what I can do or what I can become. All I knew was this feeling of being a robot waking up rushing in the morning, going to work, getting the job done and then going home. And I enjoyed being that robot. That was me. That was my life. And now, I am just this robot not knowing what to do in this unfamiliar place, as if my programming is not for this environment. My system is shut down. This nice lady I met here in Yellowknife told me that I had been brainwashed by society, that I should not feel less valuable just because I am not producing, because I am not making money. She said, "Focus your energy on your children. It's a beautiful energy. Once you do this, you will know who you really are. Shed those artificial parts and the real you will come out."

Now that I think hit the right spot. It is about balance and accepting who I really am inside. With me, motherhood is not the only source of my fulfillment because I know in my heart that I am the best mother I can be and yet I still feel that something is missing. I want to do something big, something bigger than me. But I don't know what yet. I usually and easily fill this void by shopping. If only there was a shopping mall here where I could really shop. Wal-Mart? I am not thinking clearly anymore. I am such a mental wreck. I am a robot having a malfunction. Oh my goodness, what if I have that illness? What is it called? My sister told me about it, something about winter, about not getting enough sun. I can't remember what it is called. Darn. I should go out tomorrow to get some sun. How can I go out when I will still be so tired because I haven't slept? I hate this. Damn it, why can I not go to sleep?

I think of getting up again and drinking more wine but decide that it's best for me to stay in bed. I hide under the covers to block the light coming from the iPhone.

"Why are you still awake? Are you all right?" he whispers as he hugs me.

"I think I need a break away from this place. The move and me being a stay-at-home mom is getting to me. I think a visit to my mother and my sister will help," I say. "I miss them. I want to do a lot of walking and shopping. I want to go to a real shopping mall with lots of people and stores. I miss TTC and the Eaton Centre. And I miss Starbucks. I want to have café mocha—a good café mocha."

"When?" he asks.

"Next week. Friday. Oh, and I want to go to a spa. I want to have my nails done. I want to have a massage too."

"We'll see."

"Really? Oh, I'm going to eat sushi, a lot of sushi. A sushi buffet. I'm going to visit my friends. And I am going to buy some groceries too that I can bring back here."

"Don't be too excited. We are not sure about this yet."

"Why not?"

"Money. We'll have to see if we can afford it."

"I can use my credit card. Oh, I wish I could go. I could attend my nephew's baptism. My mom and my sister would be so happy."

"And you will be happy again. Do you really need this break?"

"Yes, I do. I think I need to get a breather away from here even for just a short while. Don't be angry with me when I am depressed. I am not angry with you. I am working hard to be at peace with this place. It is difficult for me but I know I can get through this. You are the only reason why I'm here. Keep me happy. Don't drive me away."

He kisses me and softly whispers, "Sorry."

I kiss him back. Slowly, I feel his tongue passionately wanting to be inside my mouth. I feel him pulling me closer, his arms wrapping around my body. I run my fingers through his hair, down to his neck, to his chest. I kiss him on his lips as I caress his chest then his shoulders. I nibble his right ear and work my way down to his nipples. I know that I have only been here in Yellowknife for six months and that I don't know how or what the days will bring but at this moment I realize—I am blessed with one thing that is certain—that no matter what happens my heart is with this man and I will survive anything for us.

JANUARY GO, author of *For Us*, rekindled her love of writing when she moved to Yellowknife in 2010 with her husband and three sons. A member of Northwords NWT, she enjoys writing poems, children's stories, and blogging about motherhood. *For Us* is January's first published work.

Children of the Strike

by Jamesie Fournier

Growing up, my father was a miner at Giant Mine in Yellowknife and on strike during the violent labour dispute of the '90s. I always regarded my father as a free-thinking radical fighting against an oppression threatening not only himself but the community as well. I loved accompanying my father as he went about his days through the community and I felt proud that so many people knew him and regarded him well. Those years during the strike were some of the happiest days that my brother and I can remember.

In the summers during the strike my father would coach our softball team, and in the winter he coached my brother's hockey teams. On top of this he played in his own fastball and hockey leagues. My dad was home and made us lunch to come home to from school, and my mother became the breadwinner of the family. My brother and I accompanied our father on the picket line whenever school was out. These days were fun. We would picnic out there with the very zealous, angry protestors on the picket line or safe in the confines of the Union Hall and play make-believe with the other children of the strike. I remember the summers of '92 and '93 cheering on every Blue Jays game of the World Series with our father in the Union Hall, drinking coffee and feeling very mature.

Christmas parties were organized and hosted by the union for the support and benefit of the families caught up in the financial disasters of the labour dispute. There were presents for every child and my brother and I played, feasted, sang, and compared presents with all the other children. I still remember getting our pictures taken with Mr. and Mrs. Claus each year and then coming home and tacking them up on the Canadian map we had on the wall beside the kitchen table where we had our family meals and where our parents played cards religiously.

In the summers we had beach barbeques, cookouts downtown, and various rallies of protest and support. The beach barbeques were always the best; the grown-ups sat around, ate, and talked amongst themselves. My brother and I usually spent the better part of those days eating, playing with the other children, or learning how to play horseshoes with the other strikers.

One summer day on the picket line the road to Giant was mottled with signs of protest and violent anger. Wrecked satellite dishes and fallen power poles were juxtaposed with the golden locks of Miss Piggy from the Muppets, wearing only underclothing and swaying in the breeze from a hangman's noose, eyes and snout cast downwards in an expressionless stare. It was a symbol of the hatred and contempt for Royal Oak Mines owner Peggy Witte.[1]

That day school was out, and my brother and I stationed ourselves in a makeshift watchtower that had been erected on top of a burned-out school bus. We were outfitted with various binoculars and telescopes to keep watch on the encroaching lines of the horizon, and we kept an eye out for any signs of trouble, whether it was police, crews of scab-labourers complete with Pinkertons,[2] or both.

There, perched up in this tower, beyond the southern horizon, my brother and I observed faint, hallucinatory, whirling flares, dissipating in the noon hour glare, flickering in amber-whites and pale rubies. Our breaths quickly shortened as we recognized a sight we were only familiar with second-hand through our father.

Hostile images of riot police clubbing with the rhythmic cant of war drums across their shields ran swiftly through our minds. Haunted

---

[1] Now Margaret M. Kent

[2] Paramilitary anti-labour, strikebreaking security organization with a long history of violent union busting, hired by Royal Oak to guard the Giant mine, company executives, and scabs.

tales of savage maulings at the jaws of German-shepherds possessed our thoughts with images of tooth and claw tethered loosely to cowardly men in gas masks and full riot gear. Gnashing and gnarling their way through the toxic, sepulchral clouds of tear gas, they would tear their way viciously through the exhausted workers clad in only jeans, T-shirts, and baseball caps.

Slowly and menacingly they came, staggering in the searing aura of the summer heat. Lying on old, rough two-by-fours, we watched in silent awe as the destruction ahead of us advanced pace by pace. I was frozen in shock but my mind was racing and I wondered just how much danger we had gotten ourselves into. Quickly, my brother turned the gaze of his telescope in the opposite direction as I kept an eye upon the gathering storm in front of us. Desperately awaiting my brother's reply, my anxious and nervous heartbeats could not count the time—the clock that never strikes!

I heard my brother breathe a strained exhale as he grimaced, squinted, and contorted his vision through his telescope. Never before had he put such effort into this one task, so that it took him to the point where he absent-mindedly forgot what he was doing or even looking for! He drew in a measured breath and held it as he wet and smacked his lips while he scanned across the service roads peppered with waste rock, carved into the Canadian Shield. He exhaled and finally spoke in a surprisingly calm and casual tone.

"Yep…they're over here too."

We both now focused our attention towards the north and spied the very same lights bending, crawling their way across a sloping ridge of the broken-down highway, marching to the same dusty cadence as their counterparts, spinning and fading into sun-bleached pastels.

Our hearts sank as the futility of our situation dawned upon us. We checked and double-checked our findings, hoping to have only stumbled upon a mirage of some sort, but there was no doubt about it. They were coming. Slowly but surely they were coming. The hammer was coming down, and we were surrounded, caught smack dab in the middle.

Next my brother and I did what we should have done from the very beginning: we descended like terrified angels from our bird's nest, prophesying the coming doom and judgement headed our way.

"COPS!" The words sprang from our mouths like lightning and ignited the air as we leaped and bounded from the old burned-out school bus to our father's beaten up Ford Bronco II.

Our father had been busy making our lunch for the afternoon: cans of cool, crisp No Name ginger ale coupled with delicious egg salad sandwiches, wrapped meticulously in wax paper with mathematical precision.

He stuck his head out of the cracked, broken back door of our truck and gazed down the vacant road in quiet suspicion and alarm. His bearded, toothless maw hung open as he peered through his thick-rimmed, tinted glasses. A look of regret, concern and confusion washed over his face. Perhaps he was recalling previous protests and riots that my brother and I were not allowed to attend due to the likelihood of a violent outcome. As a result of his participation in one of these, my father had spent three months incarcerated.

"How many?" A second voice arose from the shadows, another striker answering our call with cautious apprehension.

Immediately a quote from John Connor came to mind as I thought "*All of 'em I think.*"[3] The gravity of the situation held my tongue as we stood breathlessly.

"Lots." I replied.

"Down both sides!" my brother gasped.

We were instructed to fetch the binoculars and we flew like panicked birds up the tower and dived back down with the swift precision of predators, urgently relaying our prey back to our handlers. Binoculars grasped, the strikers stepped eagerly out into the open.

---

3 See *Terminator 2: Judgment Day*

My father's arthritic gait, due to twenty-five years working underground, made his steps seem all the more lively as he limped his way out into the open road. And there the two men stood silently, facing opposite directions as if waiting for the other to turn and draw. My father stared off into the oblivion ahead, unwilling to believe what was coming down upon us. The other striker grumbled obscenities underneath his breath as he gazed down the sun-stroked highway.

As I stood standing there waiting, panicked in that old chalky air, anxious and out of breath, the memories of the day my brother and I had not been allowed to accompany our father to the picket line surfaced again.

It had started one day at the beach at one of the union's barbeques. Our dad had told us there would be another protest the next day. My brother and I were excited at this news and decided to make signs for the occasion. That following day my brother and I waited for our father to come home and pick us up. We had our coats, shoes, hats and signs ready when he finally walked in the door, but something was different. He arrived with a flustered, concerned, and stern look on his face. Something had changed his usual calm and warm demeanour. When he explained to my brother and me that we couldn't go with him we were crushed. We cried and begged for him to let us come along despite the consequences, but he turned to us in a troubled parental tone and explained: "It's going to be too dangerous for you guys and I won't be able to look after you!"

My mother came around the corner asking what was going on; the commotion and confusion was pulling her apart at the seams. My father explained it again to her.

"There's probably going to be a fight," he added.

"I can't bring the boys out there, it's not safe, they could get hurt." He tried consoling my mother with these last words but it just unnerved her even more. She tried to convince him to stay home, but his mind was already made up. Royal Oak had made it for him and all of the other strikers as well. The company had drawn first blood and crossed that line long ago. The protest was a powder keg lit by Royal Oak and he needed to be there when it went off.

Afterwards, at home, the aftermath of that day played out heavily upon our family. My father gathered my brother and me and explained that things were going to change dramatically for us. He explained that the protest had turned into a riot and people had been hurt. He told us that he was probably going to jail, for how long he didn't know. As a family we were devastated, and a feeling of helplessness and defeat would begin to haunt our daily lives. My father gave us only vague descriptions of what had happened that day, not wanting us to become involved or to worry for him and, as a family, we left it at that and began to come to terms with the reality of our situation. We were going to be alone.

That night my father put us to bed and read to us the adventurous tales of "Burglar" Baggins, who joined a team of angry, dispossessed dwarves setting out to destroy a monstrous and marauding dragon in order to reclaim what was rightfully theirs. Our minds slipped away as we battled bravely against giant evil spiders, and saved our comrades with our mighty dagger—*Sting*! Our father left us with dreams of Middle Earth and I listened as he returned to our mother and began to recount what had happened that day at Giant.

Everything had started at the main gate. That was where the picketing post was with the burned-out school bus and tower. One hundred and fifty strikers, steelworkers, and union supporters had gathered, rallying and protesting. The RCMP's Emergency Response Team had already set up roadblocks barricading any entrance to or from the mine from the highway. The RCMP's specialized riot troop could not arrive on time due to miscommunication, an error which the RCMP would soon come to regret.

Inside the inner gate of mine property, Royal Oak's Pinkerton riot team, Sierra, awaited in full gear for the strikers. A Royal Oak bus carrying strike-breakers, mine executives, and Pinkertons approached the main gate. The bus had the option of leaving the property at an entrance where striking was prohibited, yet they chose the main gate in spite of the demonstration. The bus, however, cleared the protestors without incident with the aid of picket-line co-ordinators.

Through the open entrance picketers rushed the company's parking lot to the inner gate. Rocks and insults flew back and forth almost immediately between the strikers and Pinkertons as tempers began to flare.

"Let them come!" yelled the RCMP's ERT operations commander to the Sierra team as strikers charged from the entrance to the inner gate. A wire on the gate was cut and strikers rocked it back and forth until they brought it down.

"Now!" A loud voice boomed over the commotion.

As if on cue, the ERT operations commander threw a concussion grenade at the strikers, which exploded in a deafening bright flash as one striker stood over top of it, badly burning his leg. The ERT team then began hitting picketers with tear gas and grenades as attack dogs and handlers quickly retreated. Members of the Sierra team soon retreated as well and ran and hid for cover as the miners kept coming undaunted, even more furious than before.

Chaos ensued as fifty or so strikers flooded the inner gate. The Sierra team, now separated and scattered, ran for cover wherever they could with strikers in close pursuit. A group of Pinkertons fled to a nearby catchment pond, behind a suppressing fire of tear gas and concussion grenades. Strikers pursued and began throwing the canisters of tear gas and grenades right back at the joined forces of police and Pinkertons. One of these strikers was my father, Jim Fournier.

A Pinkerton guard in full riot gear ran away and collapsed in the nearby pond. The ERT operations commander drew his weapon as he watched protestors approach his fallen soldier. The commander raised his gun and took aim and was about to shoot my father in cold blood when, at the last moment, other protestors stumbled into his line of sight and blocked his shot. Instead, he fired two warning shots into the air. My father, who did not hear the warning shots, now stood towering over the guard lying in the shallow pond and began to berate him for being a coward and failing to defend his friends. The operations commander fired two more warning shots at my father as he began to lift a large rock into the air. With the rock in his hands now well above his head, my father paused and then threw the rock down to the ground. The rock landed to the side of the guard, scaring and splashing him. The guard then got up out of the water and fell to the ground nearby, unconscious.

When the RCMP's riot team finally arrived on the scene the violence of the situation had already begun to die down. Armed with snipers, M-16s, and attack dogs, the riot police stood ready with pistols drawn, ready to fire. The riot team took formation at the highway parallel to the main entrance and began marching into the already badgered and bloody strikers. Two RCMP members assaulted a pregnant woman, and left her bloody in a taxi cab for the hospital. The riot team continued in this cold-blooded, violent fashion until they had shut the whole place down.

All these images and memories replayed over and over again in my mind as my brother and I waited for our father and the other striker to make sense of the approaching fury coming down upon us. We watched the threatening flashes of light that surrounded us close in, drawing the noose tighter and tighter around our necks. I began to regret not coming down and warning them sooner; we would have had more time to call in for help, to prepare, to steel ourselves. We would have had a chance.

My father strained a sigh and lowered his binoculars and handed them to us as he turned and walked away with an aggravated and pained look on his face.

"You guys...." The three of us snapped our heads around and inclined our ears, anxious and afraid of our next move.

"It's a parade!" My father barked at us in a familiar tone of mock annoyance as he limped back into the shadows. My brother and I stood dumbfounded and confused while the grown-ups went back to their posts relieved, cackling and swearing away while they wiped their brows in amusement.

My brother and I still stood speechless in the middle of the road and looked down both sides of the highway feeling vacant and bewildered. As we peered through the lenses we saw a maddening crowd, which included police, but was comprised of large groups of people. Through our binoculars we could see them all: mothers, children, city notables, and friends.

The police were chaperoning what I would later find out to be the Union of Northern Workers Tri-Annual Convention, which was being held in Yellowknife that year. The union had organized a walk down to the picket line from both ends of the city, with everyone carrying signs promoting civil liberty and justice. The union, the strikers and their families, and other members of the community had marched on the mine from different corners of the city in moral support of the strike and in protest against the violent anti-labour campaign employed by Royal Oak. The police were only there to ensure the safety of everyone.

It was a demonstration of support and unity in the face of adversity and oppression. It was a warm reception filled with laughter and strength. There were so many people it was hard to move around as my brother and I waddled through the crowd, searching out all the other children present so we could relay to them the surprise, and fear we had felt as we watched them ominously approach. Songs of perseverance were sung and Royal Oak witnessed the strength, determination, and spirit the whole union possessed as a unit and as a family. They watched us as we stared right back at them.

In the end the strike was never resolved, and nine men were ultimately murdered at the hands of one member of the CASAW Union,[4] Roger Warren. When Giant finally shut down years after the strike, the city took on the temporary air of a ghost town until diamonds

---

4 Canadian Association of Smelter and Allied Workers

were discovered in the north. People soon forgot about *Yellowknife—Where the gold is paved with streets.*

Twenty years later there is still one thing that has always perplexed me. It is a piece of graffiti still visible today. Shortly after the explosion at Giant, on the side of a former stationery store in downtown Yellowknife, someone had spray painted *CASAW KILLERS!* in plain sight so that anyone driving downtown could not possibly miss it. Eventually, the word *KILLERS!* was painted over so it just read *CASAW* with a big red block beside it.

It has weathered years of harsh conditions of the north, and no one has ever thought to clean up the graffiti or simply have the whole thing painted over. You can still approach this wall and, with the right vision, still feel and breathe the emotions etched into the side of our city and be transported back to that bleak era of its history. The irony of this graffiti is that in present-day Yellowknife it graces the side of the head office of one of the prominent diamond mines in the NWT.

Perhaps it is the city's subconscious unwillingness to forget, to keep a visual reminder to perpetuate its own sense of communal guilt and depression, or simply just the callous indifference or obliviousness of the corporate mining industry to the history, values, and morals of its own workforce.

The Giant Mine Strike goes down as one of the worst catastrophes in the north. It will remain a significant memory in the conscience of everyone who was ever involved. The passion and the pain will remain in the backdrop of the community indefinitely and will forever be carved into the city's identity.

JAMESIE FOURNIER, author of *Children of the Strike*, is a student in the Bachelor of Education Program at Aurora College in Fort Smith. He was born and raised in Yellowknife, studied film at Carleton University, and gained an interest in creative writing at thirteen when he began writing poetry. He grew up with a passion for comic books and horror

films, which left him with a deep appreciation for detective and horror fiction. He works as a part-time librarian and spends his free time reading Michael Connelly and Stephen King. It was Frank Miller's *The Dark Knight Returns* that drew him to storytelling as his own personal Dark Tower. *Children of the Strike* is his first published story.

Where They Belong
by Jessie C. MacKenzie

*I would like to dedicate this story to all of our loved ones who
lost their lives to the lake. May your souls rest in peace.*

When I was young I fell in love with a fisherman. He spent most
of his life out on the lake with his family; his mother was Chip,
like us, from Deninu Kue and his father was Scottish. He, his parents,
and three brothers, they were nice people, always smiling and laughing... probably because they ate so much good fish. The deep water
fish from the East Arm is the best, everyone knows that. Some people
say we're spoiled, but I don't think so, we're just lucky... or maybe
we know how to fish better than other Dene!

Liam was his name, he was the second youngest. Tall and strong,
he was the handsomest brother and his father's favourite. When I
would visit the fish camp he would cut out all the cheeks for me, I liked
to eat those the most, still do. I thought I would marry him one day.

When they got older, he and his brothers would leave the fish
camp and go to town, to Yellowknife. They should have stayed, they
got into all sorts of trouble when they left. "You boys are better off
out on the lake, that's where you belong!" I heard their father yelling.
Still, Liam was always smiling and laughing, having a good time. I
didn't care about any of the stories I heard about him. Not even when
I didn't see him for two years. You can't say that person is no good if
you don't know where their heart is.

He was in jail in Yellowknife. I guess some people go crazy when
they're in the city for too long, I used to be scared to go there. Those
boys kept on getting into trouble. When they would come back home

it wasn't the same, no more smiling or laughing. Sometimes the RCMP would even come to to Lutsel K'e and ask questions, look for them. I wished they would come back....

I remember when the first brother died, Don. He froze to death on the ice road to Detah. He wandered off onto the lake alone and passed out. You never go anywhere by yourself at night, no wonder he died. Too much alcohol, he wasn't thinking straight. Two years later their other brother died. His boat capsized and he didn't know how to swim. None of them did ... think about that, a family of fisherman and not one of them could swim! It was really sad, times were hard for that family. I was all grown up by then, out of La Point Hall and about to marry your father. Liam would write me letters though, and send me dream catchers he made. That's what a lot of those prisoners would do I guess, to keep busy, at least they were doing something. His mom told me he was finally coming back home. He would stay for a while, it was fun for everyone, he fed me cheeks like he used to when we were kids.

But again and again that Liam always ended up back in Yellowknife, or other places down south. After that, he didn't look so strong and handsome anymore, the city was really getting to him. People were even afraid to go to the fish camp, his parents moved to Fort Chip, everything changed. I carried on though with my life.

More time passed. These Cree girls from Manitoba, relatives of your grandpa, came to visit for the gathering at Reliance. We invited them to stay with us in Lutsel K'e for the fall. They told me a story while we were berry picking. It was almost supper, the sun was setting when an owl swooped down right in front of me, about two feet away. Maybe it wanted my berries, I don't know. I didn't think much of it, they can be peculiar animals. I only wanted to get back to the house and have supper, didn't make a big deal, not even when it started making noise and screeching. One of the Cree girls said that because I saw an owl at night, someone I knew would die soon. I laughed at them, *eschia*! Sounded like nonsense to me.

Three weeks later Liam died. I guess those Cree girls knew something after all, and I felt guilty for laughing at them. He was out on the lake checking nets, what he'd been doing his whole life. No one knows how it happened, some say he slipped and hit his head, others say the lake spirits took him. I think the lake took him myself, he was too smart to make clumsy mistakes. Better to die out on the lake than in jail or in some strange city down south. The old man's words were true, his sons did belong out on the lake. But you know what my girl? I never stopped loving Liam.

The youngest brother, David, he's still alive, the last one left. We saw each other when I was in town for your cousin Jimmy's wedding. "Marie I have something to give you! Liam forgot it at my house last time he was here, he meant to give it to you," he said. David dragged me out of the Elks, down the road to trail's end, into the tiniest trailer I've ever seen, just pitiful. He was rummaging through a dresser drawer that had empties stacked on top. I hoped that whatever he was looking for didn't smell like beer. Finally he pulled it out, this dream catcher that I hang from my bedroom window. White hide, white feathers, two nice big eagle feathers, shells, and shiny silver beads, four dream catchers made into one...the biggest with two smaller ones on either side, then the last at the bottom, real fancy—I think it's his best work. Did you notice he used a different kind of pattern that looks like nets? You say it's the nicest dream catcher you've ever seen, and I agree. I know you really like it, but I can't give it to you my girl. It was a gift from my old friend, made just for me. But if you really want one for your own house, we'll make one together. Go get me my sewing box and beads.

JESSIE MACKENZIE, author of *Where They Belong*, was born to a Dene/German mother and a Scottish/Lakota father. Spending the summers in Windsor and the school year in Yellowknife, she enjoyed both the city life and northern life. As a typical northerner, she regularly went boating and ski-dooing, tagged along on hunting trips, and attended drum

dances. Being very close to her grandmother Celine Conrad and her great-uncle Alex Desjarlais, she would always ask them to tell her stories of the "old days." Thus, storytelling and creative writing came naturally and is something Jessie has been doing since she was seven years old. Now in adulthood and attending the University of British Columbia studying political science and theatre, she makes it a rule to take time out and write stories with northern content as a means to stay connected to her Dene roots.

Acknowledgements

For many years the idea of publishing an anthology of writing from the Northwest Territories was only a dream. The dream became a reality when De Beers Canada, the Premier Sponsor of NorthWords NWT, caught our enthusiasm and agreed to fund the project as part of the company's commitment to supporting literacy in the Northwest Territories. We are grateful to De Beers, and in particular to Terry Kruger and Cathie Bolstad, for helping us realize our dream.

This anthology features the work of seventeen northern writers, some of whom have never been published before. The stories were selected from a total of ninety-four submissions. We at NorthWords feel that the success belongs not only to those who had their stories selected for publication but to all those who submitted. For a writer, often the most onerous part of the process is getting the words down on the printed page and all those who submitted succeeded in that vital first step. We thank and congratulate you all.

We would also like to thank John Mutford and Judy McLinton for reading the submissions and making the final selections. To Catharina de Bakker, Maurice Mierau and all the staff of Great Plains Publications for editing the stories and publishing the book, thank you. Thank you also to Yellowknife photographer Dave Brosha for the stunning image on our cover. Finally, we'd like to thank NorthWords Executive Director Annelies Pool who had the vision to publish this anthology and used her enthusiasm and organizational skills to push the project through to its completion.

David Malcolm, President,
NorthWords NWT